These stories are a work  incidents are fictitious and any similarities to actual persons, locations, or events is coincidental. This work cannot be used to train artificial intelligence programs.

No AI tools were used in the writing of this book or to produce the artwork thereon.

ISBN: 978-1-998763-41-2

All rights reserved.
Dark Worlds We Wander Copyright © Kristin Kirby 2024
Logos included in/on this volume Copyright © 2024 Unnerving

Cover art by Chris Bivins.

TUMBLE originally appeared on the *NoSleep Podcast* in 2024, BEING FROM ANOTHER WORLD originally appeared in *365tomorrows* in 2016, MEAT originally appeared in *Negative Space 2: A Return to Survival Horror* from Dark Peninsula Press in June 2023, SOJOURN originally appeared in *365tomorrows* in 2016, FLY originally appeared in *MYTHIC* magazine in Summer 2018, FALLEN originally appeared in *365tomorrows* in 2016, THE EDITOR originally appeared in *365tomorrows* in 2018, BITTY originally appeared in *Murder Park After Dark: Vol. 3* in October 2020, DIGESTIBLE originally appeared in *365tomorrows* in 2016, BLUNDER originally appeared on *The Overcast* podcast in 2020, MAZE originally appeared in *SERIAL* magazine in January and February 2020

Dedication

To my father and my sister.

DARK WORLDS
WE WANDER
KRISTIN KIRBY

Imprints	9
Tumble	19
Being from Another World	25
Meat	27
Lost Classics of the '90s	39
Sojourn	67
Fly	70
Fallen	83
The Nyx Effect	85
The Editor	117
Bitty	119
Digestible	125
Blunder	125
Rabbit	141
Maze	149

IMPRINTS

Cherise texts me. It's late and I'm half-asleep. She says she's coming down with something. She feels all achy.
    I text her back. 'R U still going with me?'
    In the morning I'm getting my first tattoo, and Cherise is supposed to come with me for support. I'm afraid of needles. Cherise has dozens of tattoos—sea turtles and butterflies and colorful flower designs. Her left arm is covered in a sleeve of bright orange koi, all intertwined. She's my tattoo heroine.
    'Can't,' she replies. 'Sorry.'
    Determined to not be a weeny, I go alone.
    Dez has black ear plugs the size of nickels and a tattoo of a rattlesnake coiled along his upper arm next to a saguaro cactus. I'm shaking as he begins, but the two and a half mini bottles of vodka I chugged in the car finally kick in and I barely feel the sting. I know Dez can tell my eyes are glazy, but he doesn't say anything. As he works, he's funny and patient. He cranks the tunes and we listen to The Cure and I end up having a great time.
    "When I was a kid," I tell Dez, feeling in my cups, "my parents bought me a little gray mouse from the pet store. I named her Perky, and she would sit on my shoulder while I fed her sunflower seeds. Sometimes she'd sniff my ear

and her whiskers would tickle."

Dez tells me he has a ferret named Bill.

I smile at that and keep going. "My mom died that summer. It was a hard summer. But I had my little mouse to take care of to keep me distracted. And she kind of took care of me too, you know?"

I realize I'm talking a lot, but Dez doesn't seem to mind. Pretty soon he picks up a mirror and asks, "Wanna see it?"

His detail is exquisite, and the plump brown-gray mouse he creates on my shoulder looks just like Perky. She sits on her hind legs and looks out at me with soulful eyes, little paws held close and ears as delicate as rice paper. Her tail twines around her rump with just a hint of end curl. Dez takes pictures with my phone before he puts gauze and tape over the tattoo. It looks pretty raw.

"Leave the gauze on for at least twenty-four hours," he says. "No peeking."

I give him an impulsive hug before I leave.

In the car, I text Cherise the best picture of my tattoo before I drive out of the parking lot. She doesn't respond the whole day, and I figure she's really sick. Finally around 9:00 my phone beeps. I'm glued to *Unsolved Mysteries* and don't check it for a while.

'Love it!' Cherise has said, with a thumbs-up and a heart.

I feel like a bad friend for waiting so long. 'How R U feeling?' I text back. 'Need anything? Chicken soup?'

'I'm OK.'

'Dez is great,' I text. I add an emoji of a mouse. Cherise doesn't reply.

Two days later I finally get her to have lunch with me.

"You must have really caught something horrendous," I tell Cherise as she sits down across from me. She looks pale, and even though it's like 80 degrees and we're at an outdoor table in the sun, she keeps her cardigan on over her tee.

Cherise's gaze goes to my shoulder. I'm wearing a tank top so I can show her my tattoo. "So?" she asks.

I laugh and twist in my chair. "Isn't it cute?"

Cherise leans across the table to get a better look. "Just the one?"

"I might get another one, but I'll never catch up to you."

Something troubled scuds across her face like a cloud across the moon, but she covers with a smile. "Be careful not to be in the sun too long, especially when it's new."

I remember Dez saying something about that. I slip my jacket over just that shoulder.

"I thought I'd be stressed about doing it," I say, "but now I feel so…I don't know, like it was the right thing, you know?"

Cherise shifts uncomfortably in her chair, not meeting my eyes. Then she says, "At first, they made me feel good. More than just the endorphins—with every new one, it felt right. Like you said. Even now when they've become so many. I mean, people have been getting tattoos for centuries, right? And it's all okay. We still have free will. Right? But do we?"

Amused, I try to follow her train of thought. "Yeah, who has free will anymore anyway?"

Cherise doesn't answer, just stares at her hands.

By our second glass of wine, Cherise has a sheen of perspiration on her face and she takes off her sweater. Her arm glows iridescent orange, crowded with fat koi jostling for room.

"Gorgeous! Did you get more fish?" I reach out to touch her tattoos.

Cherise flinches away. "I'm still not feeling well," she mumbles as she stands and jerks her sweater back on. "You don't mind, do you?"

Alarmed, I reach for my car keys. "Should I drive you home?"

"It's okay."

Cherise was always the cool one in our college clique. I was always the nerd. I don't fawn over her like some of our school friends, but I like hanging out with her. She's not always the warmest person, but her behavior in the past few days has been more offish than usual, and it hurts.

That night the tattoo stings like it's had too much sun. I gently press a baggie of ice to my shoulder and debate whether to text Cherise. I finally decide if she wants to talk, she'll initiate.

In the morning, I do the two-mirror trick to look at my tattoo and almost drop the hand mirror. There's what looks like another mouse, another tattoo, peeking out from behind the first one—but less detailed and formed, like it's a mistake Dez tried to cover up. Why hadn't I seen it before? I stare at it from all angles. It's hard to catch, but it's there.

I drive back to Dez's, but when I get there he's finishing up with a customer. I fume as I wait at the counter. I sneak a swig from the last mini bottle of vodka I'd gotten from the car. Liquid courage. I hate confrontation.

Dez is all smiles when he comes out from the back. "How's it going? Amy, right?"

I just turn around and slide my jacket from my shoulder to show him. Then I turn to face him. "I think I want a refund."

He gives me a blank look. "Hey, you go somewhere else after me, that's not my business."

Somewhere else? I twist and peer at my shoulder in the mirror behind the counter. The second mouse seems more in view than before, not peeking out but now next to the first mouse. It's almost as cute as my Perky tattoo but not as sharply detailed.

"You did it, right?" I ask. "This second one? Why—"

"I did one, like we agreed. You saw it."

Dez is getting pissed. He absently rubs his arm, where there are now a half-dozen saguaro cactuses practically hiding the rattlesnake.

I try again. "If you didn't do it, how did it get there?"

He just stares at me. Now I'm not sure what happened. Had I blacked out on mini vodkas and gotten another tattoo somewhere else?

Dez says, "Your friend Cherise was here yesterday, like you, ranting about her tattoos. I'm an artist and an honest person. I don't appreciate the accusations."

I want to ask Dez about his arm, why so many more cactuses. But he only nods toward the door.

As I head through the mall to the exit, I notice so many people with tattoos, not just one, but full arm and leg sleeves. Or shoulders, necks, chests, people's entire backs. Skulls and flowers and faces and crosses. Abstract designs and symbols and names and sayings and scenes from movies. And animals, so many animals.

But it's the teenage kid getting pizza at Sbarro who makes me stop dead. Along his neck there's a tattoo of a black dragon with a spiky tail. As the kid waits at the counter for his order, I can swear I see the dragon's tail twitch and rise from his skin into the air—for a second there are two tails—then slide back under. Like there's another dragon under the first one.

If I could see it from across the mall, the kid must have seen it. Or at least felt it. But he just scrolls his phone, looking bored. The couple in line behind him don't react either.

I text Cherise from my car, but she doesn't reply. My

shoulder stings again. I twist toward the rearview mirror and crank my head. Two pairs of bright mouse eyes stare back at me. Maybe Cherise knows something. Maybe that's why she confronted Dez. I decide to drive to her place and find out.

Lazy red lights flash from an ambulance in front of the house Cherise rents. I park across the street and death-grip the wheel to stop my hands from shaking. Was she really this sick? And I didn't help her.

Two EMTs wheel a gurney out Cherise's open front door. She's mostly covered in a sheet, one bare arm out, the tattooed one not visible. The sheet is stained with blood. I jump out of my car, don't feel my legs as I run to Cherise, don't feel my hands as I grab her bare arm. I'm gasping, not able to get enough air.

From the gurney, Cherise turns terrified eyes to mine. "Amy…" Her voice is barely a squeak. Her hair is plastered to her head, streaked in sweat and blood.

"What happened?"

"Ma'am," one of the EMTs says, "we have to hurry."

I let Cherise's arm slip through my hands as they wheel her to the ambulance. She tips her head back to me, not breaking my gaze. I follow.

"There were so many…" she says.

"Cherise?"

"They hide. Mimic. They spread…"

Her other arm comes out, wrapped in bloody bandages.

She points toward her house. Then she's hoisted into the back of the ambulance.

I don't remember walking in the front door, but then I'm in the foyer and I notice splashes of red to my right. The kitchen. Spatters of blood on the counter, on the cabinets. A small, wet sound, something moving. I wander farther into the kitchen.

In the sink is a serrated knife covered in blood. And on the floor by the sink, a huddled mass of bloody skin writhes like it's alive, crackling wetly. Impossibly, the bloody, squirming things are Cherise's tattoos—blue butterflies, green sea turtles, orange koi. One koi escapes the pile, twists and flops, little mouth gaping, making wet, red trails on the tile. I jam a hand to my mouth to stop a scream.

Under my jacket, little nails scrabble at my shoulder, like from a panicked animal clawing for a hold. I stumble away from Cherise's kitchen toward the front door.

I make it home in a daze and yank off my jacket, rush to the bathroom to look in the mirror. Two mice with soulful eyes look back at me, but I know one is mimicking. I rake it with my own nails, dig in, claw repeatedly, a scream building in my throat—

"Get off! Get off me!"

Until a brown-gray squirming thing the size of a mouse is flung from my shoulder to the tile floor. It lands with a plop, lies stunned a moment, then scrambles on tiny mouse feet to the corner where it huddles, shivering.

In the mirror I see only the tattoo of Perky, the one Dez did, still on my shoulder. My bare, scratched skin next to the tattoo twinges like a phantom limb, wanting to be filled.

I sit on the tub and study the creature on the floor as it shivers and breathes. Its dull eyes are half-closed, its body pressed to the wall lopsided and not quite three-dimensional, not fully formed yet.

It's dying, I realize. It just wants to live. It just needs a host.

Maybe they hide among your tattoos and mimic them so they can live. Maybe they lull you, make you feel good, make you not remember. And they start spreading. Like the cactuses on Dez's arm. Like Cherise's koi. They just keep spreading, invading, like a virus. Maybe a few people realize what's happening. Cherise realized, and it scared her.

The little creature makes a small sound. I slide to the floor and lean my face close, hear it wheezing. It's almost dead. It needs the warmth and nutrients of a host.

I reach out my finger and run it along the creature's back. It feels soft, like fur.

No, not a host. It needs someone to take care of it.

If I keep it, will I forget and think it's just another tattoo? Will there be more? Will they invade until they cover me?

Its eyes close. It gives a shudder.

I pick it up. It fits just in my palm, snug. I bet if it sat on my shoulder, its whiskers would tickle my ear.

I just want one. I just want her. Will she know that?

The twinge again from my shoulder. Empty. Wanting.

I reach back and place the creature against my flesh where she was before, hold her gently there. For a moment there's no movement. I hold my breath. Then relief as she stirs, as she slips back under my skin and flattens, settles in. She feels warm.

I carefully get to my feet and go to the mirror. I can just see the creature's outline, a shadow behind the real tattoo. She'll be safe there. I'll take care of her, and she'll take care of me. I smile as I realize it's now her eyes, warm and alive, that gaze back at me.

TUMBLE

Jenna walked out of the kitchen munching granola with almond milk and wondered when Cody had started the clothes dryer, because he was still crashed on the couch in front of a *Friends* rerun. She debated whether to wake him as a laugh track rolled over something Chandler had quipped. Then she heard another sound. A chuckling whisper that didn't come from the TV.

"Cody?"

But Cody was zonked, manspreading across the couch. Jenna set down her bowl and spoon, and there was the sound again. Coming from the laundry room. A chuckle. Or more of a gurgle. But it didn't sound like wet clothes.

In the laundry room, Jenna flipped the light switch. The ceiling's bare bulb buzzed for a second, then flickered on. The heater vent just inside the door pushed warm air onto her ankles. It was humid in the room. Jenna's bare foot squelched in water on the floor. *The washer must be leaking again.*

"Ew."

She sighed, pulled a towel from where it was wedged under the door—their doorstop—and swiped the towel over the puddle. The air from the heater slowly pushed the door, but Jenna caught it before it closed. The door liked to stick shut, especially when the room was humid. Last month she was trapped in there for an hour until Cody wandered down the hall and rescued her.

Another gurgle from the dryer. Like a wet chuckling.

Jenna peered through the round window at the tumbling clothes. They rustled and murmured in the usual way as they spun. The inside of the dryer was dark, but a film of condensation skimmed the window.

The air from the heater slowly pushed the door… Jenna lunged but missed it. The door clicked shut.

"Shit!"

Jenna grabbed the doorknob and twisted. She yanked, hard. No luck.

"Cody!" He wouldn't hear her above the heater and TV, but she gave it a shot. "Cody! The door again!"

No response.

The light bulb flickered. Jenna gave it a worried glance, stomach clenching. Cody always made sure the hall light was on when they went to bed, because he knew she didn't like the dark.

From inside the tumbling dryer came a wet thump.

What was drying in there, a giant fish? Jenna turned—

A pale, swollen hand slapped against the dryer window, fingernails jagged, crusted, dirty, then grabbed the side of the drum. Then rolling clothes blocked her view.

Jenna's heart blasted against her ribs as she tried to process what she'd seen: it was the neighbor's toddler who'd wandered in the apartment and climbed in the dryer and got trapped; it was a doll; it was a rubber hand, Cody playing a joke.

Another wet thump. Then a grunt.

But that awful hand was too big to belong to a toddler. Or a doll, or a rubber toy for that matter. And the hand had moved.

And those noises—

The light bulb went out with a zzt!

Jenna sagged against the door and moaned long and low in the pitch black. It was some *thing*, some bloodcurdling *thing*. With her in the dark.

She wrenched and yanked at the doorknob. "Please, please help!" Then she clamped a hand to her mouth. What if it heard her?

Through sheer will Jenna made her gibbering brain work. Were there words in those chuckles it made? She couldn't make out words. Were they human? If not human…then what?

What human could fit in a tiny space like that?

Jenna was safe as long as the dryer kept going, right? It couldn't get out, couldn't push the dryer door if it could only hold on as it tumbled. And it couldn't see her in the dark, right?

Did it even have eyes?

And Cody would wake up and come open the door any minute.

Unless...Cody was dead, and the thing in the dryer was coming for her next.

It killed Cody, then cleaned the blood off itself in the washer, right? Then it decided the fluff cycle would do the trick. Soon it would be dry.

But there had been no blood on Cody, and of course he was just sleeping.

So how much longer did the cycle have until it stopped? If Jenna could reset it before then, she'd have more time to figure out how to escape the room.

Jenna took a deep breath and slid around until her back was against the door. The washer and dryer were hulking squares a few feet away. She reached out a hand in the dark and found the wall. She let her fingers trail along it as she took a shuffling step toward the dryer. Then another.

Something against her fingers. Her hand encircled it— the metal rod for hanging clothes to dry. Carefully she slid the rod from its two cradles. It felt cool in her hands.

She pulled the rod to her chest as a weapon.

She took a few more steps. A few more. Almost—

BZZZZT!

Jenna jumped and shrieked. The rod clanged to the floor. The dryer was stopping. The cycle was over. The thing inside thumped hard as it did one last tumble.

Jenna whirled and lunged for the door, fists pounding.

"CODY!" she screamed. "HELP ME! CODY!" She didn't care anymore about making noise.

A click.

A shaft of light played and widened on the wall next to her as the dryer door squeaked open.

Jenna froze, tried to scream but only choked, dread stuck hard in her throat. She pressed her forehead against the door, gripping the knob so hard she knew her finger bones would break.

She heard a few grunts and thuds, a rasping, the squeezing of something bulky through a smaller opening. She heard hoarse breathing. A heavy foot slapped wetly to the floor, nails clicking.

Jenna thought, *this is it; I'm going to die*. Trapped in her own laundry room with a horrible monster thing that desperately needed a mani-pedi.

As the hysterical giggle died in her mouth, she tumbled down to a dark place, even darker than the little room she would soon be entombed in. There was only the rushing as she plunged, and it was almost comforting. She let herself free-fall.

Then a little ping found her in the dark: What about Cody? Sleeping and without a clue in the next room.

It was her turn to rescue him.

It took every drop of Jenna's resolve to come back, to bend down, feel around, and grab the metal rod. She straightened and hugged it like a lover.

She braced her hand against the door, one wild eye on the wall as the thing's dark, misshapen shadow slid along it, blocked the dryer light and then allowed it, bulbous and then flat and then bulbous again, then looming taller than she was.

Gripping the rod, Jenna squared her shoulders and turned, as the thing's other hideous foot dropped to the floor.

BEING FROM ANOTHER WORLD

They've locked me in the device like they do every time. But this time I'm putting up a fight. I scissor and kick my cramped legs, wave my arms, and the device rocks a bit. That's good. I'm stronger than before.

It was all a blur, my coming here. Images distorted and blinding, sounds loud and blaring. I was weak. Afraid. I could barely move, my limbs not used to the atmosphere, the weight.

I've acclimated a bit since then. Their language is difficult to parse, though, and so far I understand only a few words. With more time, I can crack it and communicate with them. Or maybe I'll play it close to the vest, not let them know I understand what they're saying. Keep the upper hand until I know what they intend to do with me.

I've been able to sit up, and once or twice make it to my hands and knees. I'm still unsteady; my strength soon fades and I collapse. But it's a start.

I can't clean up after myself, though. It's uncomfortable and humiliating, but what can I do? I suspect the liquids and food they force-feed me, while just enough nourishment to keep me alive, are also designed to sustain my weakened, vulnerable state. They eat their own food in front of me, but when I reach for it, they pull it away.

The door to my quarters is frustratingly close, but bars on my cage prevent my getting to it. At night they hang a contraption overhead. It rotates and makes discordant tinks and squawks. I can't figure out its purpose; I assume it's to spy on my movements and alert my keepers of any attempts at escape. I find myself staring at it for hours, wondering how I can use it for just that. Like everything else, though, they keep it tantalizingly out of my ham-fisted reach.

It's time for sustenance. And right on schedule, here comes the airplane, which usually delivers a green mush substance. Sometimes it's a train, accompanied by, from my main keeper, a hearty but unintelligible "choo choo!" But the mush never tastes like real food, and, as they don't eat it themselves, it makes me suspicious.

I try to grab the airplane, to push it away, but my hands are clumsy balloons I can't control. I bang on the surface of my device in frustration. My main keeper makes noises, waving its own long, spindly arms and baring its white teeth. It wants me to eat the mush, but I'm so angry all I can do is cry.

Eventually I get ahold of myself and open my mouth. I need nourishment, after all. This time the airplane delivers an orange substance, slightly sweet. Still only mush, but not as bad as the green stuff. I swish it around my mouth. Some dribbles down my chin, but I ingest enough to want more.

Okay. I'll eat their mush substance. I'll play by their rules. But only until I get stronger, until I can walk unaided. I'll wait for them to slip up and forget to shut the bars of my cage. Then I'll see what's out there, what new world I've been dropped into.

MEAT

Gray skies. Rain most of the day.

On our scavenge, we come across a Meat. Lucky for him. Lucky for us. He's sitting in the mud, crying. The others of his small group, what's left of them, are all dead. Surprise attack with guns and clubs, the best pieces hacked off and taken in a hurry. A small band of marauders, Brady guesses. We collect what we can ourselves, but there isn't much left.

The Meat is in shock. He keeps muttering, "They hid me. They died for me." He's grateful. He's amazed.

Brady squints at him, sizing him up. "What are you, two-twenty? Two-thirty?"

The Meat says he thinks so, last time he weighed himself. He starts to say, "My name is—" but Brady cuts him off.

"We'll take you," he says. "Okay?"

The Meat nods and starts crying again.

"I remember when Meats were three-hundred, four-hundred pounds," Dawson says. "Not that long ago."

Brady agrees. "But they were more of a liability."

And so we continue on. We're eleven now.

Night comes fast, and it gets cold. Dawson keeps watch. Some of the skinnier ones sleep next to the Meat for warmth.

He doesn't seem to mind.

I can usually handle the cold. I've got some weight left on my frame, can still pinch a little here or there. Not enough to be a Meat, but I'm okay with that.

—

Gray and overcast.

We walk all day, scavenging as we go. We don't stop to rest, and by midday the Meat says his feet hurt and his legs are cramping. But he keeps going. We position him in the middle of the group, with scouts in front and behind, and let him slow the pace. But Brady is firm about not stopping. He remembers a lake down the road. He hopes it's still there.

And it is. It's turning to mud, with a sheen of debris and ash across the surface. But the rain has replenished it a little. Once we strain out as much crap as we can and add the purifiers, the water isn't so bad. We all drink. And rest. Brady allows extra food for everyone.

Meats always get a bigger portion of food, and if there's any extra, they eat it so it doesn't spoil. When I give him the extra, the Meat thanks me. He seems less shell-shocked today. Not ready to talk much yet, but that's okay. I don't like to talk to them too much, even though we have to sometimes to make them feel more comfortable.

Dawson seems nervous. He's sent two scouts out on reconnaissance. "The marauders could be following," he tells Brady.

Brady looks unsure. "If they're still around, they would've found the Meat before we did."

"Unless they left him as bait."

That makes Brady thoughtful.

—

Hard rain all day.

We try to scavenge, but the rain is cold and biting, so we hole up in a ruined lake cottage—basically three walls with a partial roof left. Dawson finds a pile of rat bones, probably someone's old cache, and we crush them up for soup.

The kids find what look like shriveled dandelion leaves. I don't know, maybe it's crabgrass. But we throw those into the soup. "Vegetables," the kids say, and the adults laugh. The younger kids have never seen vegetables. Anyway, it's pretty good soup. We give most to the Meat, of course.

I ask him what he did before.

"I worked in a store," he says. "I was a stocker. That's of course worthless now." He asks what I did before, and I tell him I was a writer. "Oh, did I read you?"

"Only if you didn't have something better to do," I answer.

—

Gray. Always gray.

The kids seem to have more energy. They decide to check out the water for fish and frogs and birds. Most everything like that is gone, of course, but it gives them something to do.

We conduct our ceremony for the Meat in mid-afternoon, when it's a little warmer. This is the fourth ceremony we've done; Brady started them as a way to make the Meats feel welcome and significant. We all give the new Meat something of ours—something precious. We eventually get it back anyway.

I give him a silver belt buckle with a bucking bronco etched on it. I found it while scavenging. We ate the belt leather a while ago, but I kept the buckle. I like to trace the outline of the bucking horse with my fingers. It reminds me of the old days.

That night, Dawson lies down next to me and puts his hands on my breasts and pulls me against him. He's warm. We have enough energy to kiss a little. I remember in the first months, when people weren't sure if they'd survive, everyone hooked up. When I found this group, Dawson and I hit it off right away and had sex a lot. We tried to forget, tried to feel alive in each other's arms. But that was back when we still had food and energy to spare.

—

Gray. As usual.

Dawson is already up when I wake. Brady's letting the Meat sleep in. The kids are pouting because they want to see a fish and there aren't any, not even dead ones, not even bones. Nobody's in a good mood.

Later, when I wander down to the lake, just to touch a

body of water again, no matter how small or polluted, Dawson and Brady are arguing.

"The marauders could be right behind us," Dawson says.

"But we have water here," Brady answers. "It's a good place to stay for a while."

"There's no food."

"There will be. Life is attracted to water."

Dawson loses it. "What life?" he screams, waving his arms. "What life?"

And he stomps away.

We leave later that day. Dawson must have convinced Brady that if we know the location of the lake, the marauders might know too. So we fill as many containers with water as we can, and we head off.

—

Overcast. But a hint of sun.

Brady thinks it must be June or July. I lost track of the months a long time ago. But the last few days do feel warmer. And today I swear the sun is stronger through the gray sky. Brady and I talk about the weather so excitedly that Dawson snorts and rolls his eyes at us.

"It'll be at least a few more years like this," Dawson says. "Cold as hell. And then it'll all disperse and we'll roast to death from the sun. Pick your poison."

Leave it to Dawson to brighten your day.

On our scavenge, we find a tin can. It's bulging at the

top and bottom—not a good sign. The label's gone, so we don't know what it contains. But everybody is given one guess, and whoever picks the right food gets the contents. Brady opens it while we all watch. From what we figure, it's Dinty Moore stew. One of the mothers, Molly, guesses it right.

But the smell hits us right away. Something's off. Whoever eats it—well, it won't end well. We bury the can like we would a loved one. Molly tries to stay good-humored.

"I would have shared with everyone," she says. "I really would have."

—

Gray.

A very sad day. Justin, the oldest of the kids, snuck back last night and dug up the stew and ate it. A skinny little guy, and a good scavenger. But not very strong. We bury his vomit deep so the other kids won't be tempted. We know they're hungry, but this can't happen again. Molly can't stop crying. She blames herself.

Justin's hanging on, but it won't be long.

—

Later.

Justin has died. We decide to have a ceremony in his honor. Brady thinks Justin's meat will be okay as long as we stay away from the organs. Dawson mutters something about "Not enough to feed a bird."

The Meat cries as he eats.

Molly won't eat at all.

Me, I can't cry anymore, so I eat in silence.

After that, Dawson takes some of the others scavenging. The rest of us walk on for a while. The Meat has a kind of peaceful look on his face, and I ask him about it.

"I'm thinking of how lucky I am," he says. He's serious. "It's sort of beautiful, don't you think? The white frost on the ground, the bare, dark trees. I like how it's so quiet. And the way our breath fogs up in the air. That means we're breathing, right? That means we're alive."

I'm not in the mood to talk about beauty, about meaning. I'm sick of the cold, the quiet. I'm dead sick of it all. "Living and being alive are two different things," I snap.

"Maybe," the Meat says. "Maybe not. I was worthless before. I was a taker. But everything we do is important now. My life has meaning now. I'm important."

"We're protecting our food, you idiot! You're a big walking bag of fast food! That's all!"

The Meat just shrugs. He isn't even upset.

—

Gray. Overcast.

I think the sunshine was an illusion. Days go by, I don't count how many, and no sun. No rain, either. Every day we walk, we scavenge, but we don't find anything. We melt frost for water, we shiver, and we sleep. The food is all gone. No one says much. Dawson doesn't say anything and doesn't come to me at night.

Brady has a talk with the Meat. I only catch a little, but it sounds like tomorrow will be the day. "There's nothing to eat," Brady says, "and we don't know when we'll find food." The Meat takes the news well. "We give the Meats a chance to run," Brady continues. "We won't try to stop you. We do it for everyone."

The Meat says he understands. He says he won't run away.

I want to apologize to him. I want to give him something more. I don't know what. To show him I'm not completely empty inside.

—

Gray. Dark. Bad.

Marauders arrive when night falls. Six of them. They have guns with actual ammunition. We try to run and hide. Then we fight. Dawson, thank God, was keeping watch. He fights like an animal. Brady overpowers some of them, and Dawson does the rest. But the marauders kill Brady. They kill Gail and the kids. And they kill the Meat.

We'll have a ceremony later. Right now, we're gorging, regaining our strength. A lot of it will go bad, but we can eat what we want for now. And we'll keep the guns and ammunition.

Brady was a good man. I'll miss him.

I dig the silver belt buckle out of the Meat's backpack and look at it for a long time. I finally put it in my pocket.

Then I break down and cry.

—

Gray. Cold.

A long time goes by. Weeks. It's all gone and there's nothing to scavenge and everything moves by in a blur.

There are only four of us. It's hard to get up each day.

—

Maybe brighter. Maybe.

We pick up a small group. They're pretty bad off, skinnier than we are. Now we're nine. We find some outbuildings for shelter in the remains of a small town. And we find two cans of soup tucked away in a cupboard. That even gets a smile from Molly.

Dawson comes to me in the night and puts his arms around me. He whispers close to my ear. "We're going to make it," he says. Then he leaves before I can reply.

—

Gray. No rain.

Dawson has a meeting with everyone. He says we're designating a new Meat. He looks at me. I'm the least skinny, at a hundred and thirty pounds.

So I get to have a ceremony tonight. I get more food and water than the others. And everyone gives me a present. Molly gives me her favorite necklace, a gold chain with an amber pendant. She knows I've always liked it. Then she gives me a hug.

"Don't worry, it won't come to...you know," she says.

I tell Dawson I want his gun as a present so I can kill him when he falls asleep. He laughs at that, but I'll do it, I swear. Dawson says he never sleeps anymore, anyway, and he gives me his share of food for the night. He really wants to fatten me up, I guess.

I decide if I start losing weight, I won't be the Meat for long.

That's my plan.

—

Gray. No rain.

We find two people while scavenging today. They're sick and beyond help. At least that's what Dawson says. I try to give some of my food to Molly, but she only smiles and says she has enough.

I want to throw it away, but I can't. So much for my plan.

If there's an abundance of food, Meats eat it so it doesn't spoil. Otherwise, it goes to waste. It's like we're the holders of life in our bodies.

—

Brighter today, I'm sure of it.

Because I'm a Meat, I don't have to scavenge. I can rest more, which is nice. And Dawson sleeps with me every night he's not on watch. There seems to be less urgency these days, and I have time to think.

I think a lot about what the Meat told me: *everything we do is important now.*

So as I walk, I look at the frost, at the bare trees. I listen to the quiet. I hold my silver buckle up to the sky and watch the dim, hopeful refraction of light.

And I wonder, when it's my time, if I'll run. Or if I'll choose to find the beauty in the world, the meaning.

LOST CLASSICS OF THE '90S

The other night I set up our old VCR and watched one of my favorite movies: *Racer and Cap*, starring Tom Cruise and Bill Murray, from 1992. Cruise play a hotshot detective chasing drug smugglers, and Murray is a cantankerous tugboat captain who helps Cruise solve the case. Murray was nominated for an Oscar for his performance; it says so on the box. Now before you jump on IMDB to look it up, the movie's not there. As far as I know, I was the only one who had a video cassette of it. In fact, I might be the only one who'd ever seen it. At least on *this side*.

Halfway through the movie, Tim came in and sat next to me on the couch. "What are we watching?" he asked.

When I told him, he got a strange look on his face.

"Have you had this movie the whole time?" he asked.

I was puzzled at his reaction. "Yeah, it was in Charlie's boxes. From when I picked up his stuff after he moved."

"Lauren, you mean before the landlord pitched it. Charlie didn't move. He was just gone."

That brought me up short. I'd forgotten that part, Charlie disappearing without a word thirty years before. And Charlie wasn't a guy you forgot easily. If it wasn't for my storing his dusty videos and audio cassettes, I might have forgotten him completely.

While Tim took Marlowe for his walk, I stayed on the couch, not watching the movie anymore but thinking. What had prompted me to start cleaning out the basement storage room? I'd been meaning to do it for years, so why today? Charlie's boxes were stuck way back, behind old furniture, exercise equipment, knickknacks we'd been meaning to sell. I had to really dig, but I did; I dragged out everything and opened the first box that said 'Charlie' and pulled out one of his tapes.

Charlie was on my subconscious for some reason. After all these years. Because…

I stood up fast, almost spilling my beer, and headed for the kitchen.

When Tim came in the back door with Marlowe, I was on the floor digging in the recycling bag through paper and dog food cans.

"Marlowe did his business right away, hallelujah, and it started raining, so we—"

Tim paused to let our lovable, goofy, always-shedding mutt off his leash. Marlowe trotted over to me and stuck his snout in the bag, wondering what was so important. Tim came over too.

"Did I forget to rinse something?" He smiled. "I'm pretty much an expert at rinsing; I do it to people's teeth every day."

Usually I'd acknowledge my husband's humor, but I was too distracted. My hand hit what I was looking for, and

I pulled out the postcard. A few days ago I'd thought it was an ad for something and had pitched it into the recycling without a second look.

On the front was a glossy photo of a sandy beach and blue ocean. 'Wishing You Were Here? Come on Down Under!' appeared in big letters across the photo. I flipped the card over: Charlie's heavy all-caps handwriting. I remembered it like it was yesterday.

'SEE YOU SOON,' was all it said. Charlie's first contact in thirty years.

Tim peered over my shoulder. "Is he in Australia?" he asked.

I looked up at him in wonder. "Not for long."

Tim helped me to my feet. What was going on with my legs? They were shaking. Tim held my wrists and looked hard at me. "Does this mean the nightmares'll start again?"

I dodged the question, mumbling something about feeding Marlowe. Tim locked the doors and checked the windows. We went to bed early, and Tim held my hand as we lay on our backs wide awake.

"Don't be worried," I finally said. "No nightmares here."

"Uh-huh."

"You're not still jealous of Charlie."

"I'm not jealous. You really don't remember?"

"Nope." I could feel my stomach clench.

Tim rose on one elbow. "After he left, you'd talk in your sleep. Once you screamed. It was Christmas before you got a full night's rest. So yeah, I'm worried."

I moved into Tim's arms. "About Charlie? He's the least scary person in the world."

Though the first time I met Charlie in the summer of 1995, he was daunting, I'll admit. I was on break before senior year at the university half an hour from Riley. I needed to earn some money, so I got the graveyard shift stocking shelves at Kroger's. When I walked into my first night at work, I could hear Charlie's bellowing voice across the aisles as he told off another stocker who'd been sleeping on the job. Charlie was tall and kind of beefy and imposing. His hair was always shaggy, and by this time of night he had a five o'clock shadow. But when he introduced himself and showed me the ropes, he was friendly and just the nicest guy.

In fact, we shortly became good friends. We had the same taste in movies (John Carpenter and Ridley Scott) and music (The Clash). He didn't own a car, so I drove him to and from work most nights. But he always seemed to have pot, and he'd let me have some of his stash.

Our favorite thing to do after work was go for breakfast at Fitch's Five-Star diner in downtown Riley. We'd walk in the door, and like clockwork Charlie would pause and murmur in his best Alec Guinness, "You will never find a more wretched hive of scum and villainy." This usually got me laughing, which made the customers—typically truckers, townies grabbing pastries before work, and the old, wizened local farmers in overalls—stare. The old farmers were cool, though. They were there almost as often as we were, six regulars who came into town to drink coffee and shoot the breeze. Riley was a small town, surrounded by cows, corn, and soybean fields.

People thought we were a couple, but Charlie usually flirted with the waitress while I mooned over Tim, who went to the same university and was smarter than I was and carpooled with me and other students who lived in town. We'd been casually dating for a month, and I was determined to make him fall in love with me.

"What's love, anyway?" Charlie would say. "It's commitment." He'd shudder. "I like playing the field. Staying fast and loose."

I knew for a fact that "fast and loose" Charlie had a major boner for a married woman who lived in one of the nicer neighborhoods of Craftsman homes and big porches, not very far from where Tim and I lived now.

I also knew Tim didn't like that I hung out with Charlie so much. But he didn't need to worry: Charlie's favorite after-breakfast activity was for me to drive him past the married woman's house. That summer was hot, but the mornings were cool, and that's when Valerie Barton usually did her flower gardening. She was a beautiful woman, I'd give Charlie that, and she'd wear shorts and a tank top as she dug around in her roses in the front yard. Charlie would make me slow down the car as we went past, and he'd lose himself in Valerie's tanned legs and arms. She'd usually turn to look right at him and smile. Becoming shy, Charlie would tell me to drive away, and he would sigh. Their love affair from afar, never to be consummated.

As the summer went on, though, Charlie seemed more intent on after-breakfast drives out to Muck Creek Bridge. There was a stretch of woods behind the creek, and a sheep farm. I'd gone fishing there with my brothers when I was a kid. Charlie would have me stop at his place first so he could grab his camera, one of those Polaroid OneSteps that were popular back in the day. How Charlie came to know about the sheep farm was beyond me at first, but something lurked there in the grassy pasture by the woods. Something menacing.

Now, leaning next to the bedroom window so I didn't wake Tim, I looked out at the dark neighborhood street and tried to remember what that something near the woods was, but my memories had dried up. I just knew my palms were sweaty and my heart was running laps. It would be some hours before I found sleep.

—

When Charlie said he'd see me soon, he meant it. The next morning, I was picking up a coffee at Fitch's—not much had changed about the diner, except the coffee was better—and saw Charlie at our old table having a three-egg omelet. He broke out a grin and pulled me into a bear hug.

"I've dreamed about this greasy spoon for years,"

Charlie said. "How've you been?"

Charlie hadn't changed much—maybe a few thinning hairs, a few more pounds on his beefy frame. He had me catch him up on the last decades, crowing in delight when he found out Tim and I had married.

"Lauren, Tim's the luckiest guy in the multiverse. And you've broken my heart."

I chuckled. "Like you broke the heart of every waitress here?"

A new crop of old farmers, four of them, sat in their usual corner booth, showing each other pictures of their grandkids on their phones. Except one, who had to be 90, who kept staring at Charlie and me. He finally raised an arthritic finger and crooked it at us: come here.

Charlie and I went over to his table. The other farmers became silent as Charlie squatted a bit so he didn't tower over the old man.

"I remember you," the farmer said. His voice was wavery, and his eyes had the bright, filmy sheen of the very old. "Both of you."

"I remember you too, sir," Charlie said. "Coffee every morning right here."

The old farmer nodded. What he said next came out so softly we both leaned closer.

"What was that?" Charlie asked.

"Muck Creek Bridge," the old man repeated. "The farm out there. Haunted."

I almost laughed. I could tell the other farmers had heard this one too, and were amused. Townsfolk had been saying the place was haunted since I was a kid. But Charlie got a strange look on his face.

"When did this start?" he asked.

"Last week."

Charlie nodded and patted the man's shoulder as if in complete understanding.

"Thank you for telling us," Charlie said. The old farmer seemed relieved.

We headed back to our table, but Charlie was in a hurry now. He folded the rest of his omelet, shoving it into his mouth, put some money on the table, and nodded toward the door. He finished chewing by the time we got to my car. He got in like it was 1995, and I got behind the wheel.

"Muck Creek Bridge," he said.

No explanation about the farmer's comment. And Charlie didn't ask if I had any plans. It was Saturday, so I didn't have classes to teach, but I had other things to do. And Tim would want to see him. I turned to tell Charlie that. But his expression had become grim and a little scary. So I just started the car and drove.

Late September in Michigan is beautiful when the weather's warm. The trees are turning their fall orange and yellow and red, and the mellow sun on the leaves gives off this magical quality of light. As I drove, I remarked on the trees, but Charlie was preoccupied and didn't answer. I headed out of the city limits, soon got to the bridge and crossed it, and parked off the side of the road.

We got out. I could see Muck Creek winding its muddy way through shaggy trees. Grasshoppers sang in the tall, wheat-colored grass. Charlie stared in the direction of the sheep farm, surprised. The buildings were sagging, and there were no sheep. The pasture where they had grazed was overgrown.

"The sheep farmer got too old to take care of the place," I said. "They put him in a nursing home. His wife moved in with their kids in town."

"Better that way," Charlie muttered.

He headed toward the rusted barbed wire fence that was still there and carefully pushed it down, stepping over it, then keeping it down for me to step over. It was like old times, when we used to walk around here after breakfast at Fitch's. We made our way through the tall grass toward the line of small woods that bordered the creek. The sheep always used to hang out there in the shade to keep out of the summer heat. I half expected to see some—

And that's when my memory kicked back in again. In a flash, I was back on that morning in 1995, seeing those sheep, three dozen, standing in the shade of the trees, lazily watching us wander around their pasture. The farmer never seemed to mind; at least he'd never appeared from the house or farmyard. The grass was short, grazed by the sheep. I was buzzing from Fitch's coffee, even after working all night at the store, and it was July. The grasshoppers weren't singing today, and this caused Charlie concern.

"The grasshoppers got the hell out of here," he said.

We were maybe fifty feet from the creek and several yards from the sheep. Charlie's Polaroid camera hung from his neck, as usual. He kept his head down, searching the ground for something, but I'm the one who stepped on the sheep's head.

I shouted in surprise, jumping back, my ankle boot taking with it blood and gore. The kill seemed fresh, the blood not yet dry, and my first thought was coyote. There was no body—just the head, with the sightless eyes tinged blue and the long lips drawn back.

"Holy shit!" Charlie ran over, snapping photos with the OneStep, grabbing them as they rolled out. The camera buzzed and clicked.

I shook blood off my boot. "Yeah, holy shit." I was not thrilled with this, and felt bad for the poor sheep.

Something moved from behind a maple tree a few yards away, crouched low to the ground. I froze. It appeared doglike, like a coyote, as it slunk toward Charlie and me. But there was a *wrongness* about it; it wasn't furry, and it didn't have a tail. I raised my arms and made myself look big, to scare it, and took a few steps forward.

The creature straightened up to its full height, as tall as a human and shaped like one. It had arms and legs, and a head like a human's. It had hands with long fingers that ended in points. But it was naked and rubbery, and some crazy gray-green color, hard to spot at first in the grass, and its eyes blazed orange. It glared and shuffled right at me, waving its arms. I got the feeling it was frightened and overcompensating. I was scared shitless.

It kept coming at me. I yelled and stumbled back. Charlie saw the creature, muttered more oaths, and snapped pictures as it moved. I kept scuttling backward, my hands out in front of me, and the thing kept advancing. I could hear its breath coming in snorts and grunts.

"You got this!" Charlie was shouting. "It's more scared of you than you are of it!"

Was Charlie actually giving me encouragement instead of helping? He just kept taking photos, trying to get the best angle. I gritted my teeth and forced myself to quit running and become still. I growled at the creature, and thankfully it stopped short. It was as tall as I was. Its skin looked soft and fleshy, like an eel's. We stared at each other.

I waved my arms. It moved back a bit, startled.

I waved my arms again and stomped my feet. The thing leaped back with a grunt, orange eyes wide.

"What the hell is it?" I murmured to Charlie.

"Long story," Charlie replied. "Just keep scaring it."

He knew what it was? I turned to gape at Charlie then, and that was my mistake. Maybe the thing saw my looking away as a sign of weakness. With a snort it charged me.

I shrieked and tried to dodge out of the way. Its claw

hand grasped my arm, yanking. It was strong. It opened a mouth I hadn't seen before, showing hundreds of sharp needle teeth, some with sheep's wool still stuck between—

Then Charlie was there, arm raised, rock in hand, and he smashed the creature's head. The thing let go of me, wheeled drunkenly around, and Charlie hit it again. The creature went down. It didn't bleed. Nothing came out of the wounds. But it looked dead.

Gasping for breath, not really believing what was happening, I watched Charlie straighten and scan the pasture. I knew he was making sure there weren't more creatures. The sheep stayed amid the trees, not particularly panicked. This made Charlie say he thought this was the only one.

"For now," he added. He put a hand on my shoulder. "You okay?"

"You saved my life," I said. My mind was numb.

While we buried the creature, and the sheep's head with it, Charlie explained the thing came out of a portal, a door to another dimension very near this one. He said the creature more than likely would have run back to its portal if we chased it, but—he nodded toward the sheep—it had gotten a taste for meat and blood.

"We think these creatures get active every thirty or so years," he continued. "You know, like locusts? They sort of molt and start exploring. Sometimes beyond their world."

"Cicadas," I said. "Not locusts." I don't know how I

knew that.

Charlie paused. "Cicadas?"

"And every seventeen years."

He grinned. "Ah. These things are every thirty."

I was still wrapping my head around alternate dimensions as I wandered toward the maple tree the creature had been near—and almost fell into the portal. It looked like a black sliver in the air, low to the ground, roiling and shimmering like a desert mirage. A grown human could just squeeze through. Or a thing the size of a human.

My mind was blown. "This...goes to another world?" I asked. "Their world?"

"Yep. Freaky, huh?"

Charlie took some time to snap pictures of the portal and surrounding area. Then he seemed satisfied. Oh, he did one more thing; he passed some device that looked like a digital thermometer over my forehead, right there in the sheep pasture. And I pretty much instantly forgot what had just happened.

"For your protection," Charlie said.

—

But now, in the same pasture, the memory of that day in 1995 came back like a punch to the stomach. I had to lean over and take deep breaths. Charlie, ahead of me, noticed and turned. I watched his legs and sneakers walk back to stand in front of me. His jeans had dried grass seeds stuck to them.

"You disappeared that night," I said.

"I know. Sorry. I didn't want you to be burdened. And I had work to do. Figuring out a way to close this portal, and others like it. It took us a while, but we finally have something that'll work."

I was flabbergasted. "Wait. Are you like a scientist or something?"

"In my world, yes."

I straightened up fast. "In your…?"

That's as far as I got, because I realized the grasshoppers had stopped singing. Charlie noted the look on my face and nodded in grim understanding. We headed toward the maple tree, much taller now, its leaves red and orange—and the portal.

I had to know something important. "Do you come from where those things come from?"

Charlie pretended to be insulted. "God, no!" He grinned. "My world is a lot like this one. Kind of parallel, really. That's why I like it here so much."

It was hard to see in the tall grass, but we finally found the portal again. I was afraid it might be bigger or something, but it looked like I remembered: low to the ground, just a shimmering dark sliver in the air. I squatted near it to get a better look, then noticed Charlie freeze.

"Lauren," he said.

I straightened up slowly and turned to look where

Charlie was staring. Two of the rubbery, gray-green creatures were crouched a few yards away, orange eyes fixed on us.

Charlie pulled a cell phone from his pocket. I thought he was going to take pictures—fancier technology than his old OneStep—but he was pushing buttons. "Looks like we're blocking their escape back," he said quietly. "If we angle around, we can shoo them in this direction. Not that it worked so well last time."

I said, "Maybe with the sheep gone, they haven't acquired the taste for blood."

Charlie nodded at that. It reassured me. The creatures really seemed like just big, scared things that wanted to go home. I thought we might have this.

Until I saw another creature squirming its way out of the portal right next to us. First its sharp, long fingers and rubbery arms emerged. Then it shimmied its fleshy body and pulled itself out. Startled at the sight of us, it shied away from the portal toward the maple tree.

"Ah, shit," Charlie muttered.

We trotted carefully away from the portal only to see two more things crawl out, like ants from a hill. At the sight of us, they scattered in different directions. There were now five, all crouched and glaring at us.

We angled around behind the first two. Charlie raised his phone and pushed another button. Strange, cacophonous sounds erupted, like the squawks of geese combined with the honking of car horns, with a dash of smooth jazz. The two creatures reared up to full height, their attention definitely gotten. Their eyes got wider, if that was possible. They shambled in the direction of the portal, mostly to escape the awful noise.

We walked forward, keeping pace with them. Charlie held his phone in the air. The two creatures were almost at the portal when another set of rubbery arms appeared, and a sixth creature pushed its way out. The first two creatures got agitated and shuffled away from the portal.

Charlie cursed and turned off the music.

"Don't you have a gun or something?" I cried, exasperated.

Charlie gave me a look. "They don't go down with bullets. We tried shooting one on the other side. It didn't go well."

"Don't you have ray guns?"

"Ray guns? I'm not Captain Picard. I'm just on the closing-the-portal team."

"Well, what kills them? I mean, besides beating them to death?"

"Ideally we don't want to resort to more murder," Charlie said.

I was incredulous. "Murder? They're monsters!"

"To them, we're the monsters. And the longer we stay here, the more we'll rile them up and attract more to come out. Let's find a place to regroup."

We also needed some weapons, clearly. I drove us to my house. The first place we went, though, was the kitchen liquor cabinet, where we each did shots of tequila while we discussed the situation. That's where Tim found us.

Charlie gave Tim a big hug, and Tim reluctantly returned it. When they parted, Charlie noticed Tim's sour expression and grinned.

"I know you've wondered about Lauren and me. But you don't have to."

I put my hand on Tim's. "See?"

"Besides, I'm married," Charlie added.

Tim and I did delighted double-takes.

I said, "Charlie, details!"

But Charlie shook his head. "No time for that now. We have to save your world."

I wasn't sure about bringing Tim into all this. "Charlie…"

"Lauren, there are six of them," he said. "Maybe more by now. If they get too curious, they'll start moving toward town. Do you want that? What if they attack people and get a real taste for blood? I can close the portal, but we have to get them inside it first. And we need help."

We all sat at the kitchen table and explained to Tim what happened, both in 1995 and that morning, and what needed to happen next. At first Tim listened with a straight face, but that soon devolved into disbelief and then a merry twinkling in his eyes.

"You guys are so full of shit," he said, laughing. "You had me going at first too. How many tequila shots did you do before I walked in?"

Charlie looked crestfallen, not sure where to go from here. I took Tim's hands and gazed at him pleadingly.

"Sweetie," I said. "We're not making this up. We're not."

"How am I supposed to believe a story like this?"

Charlie sighed. "Let's just get some weapons and head back—"

Then I remembered something and stood. "The basement," I said. I bolted out of the kitchen.

By the time Tim and Charlie caught up with me, I was rummaging through one of Charlie's old boxes. Marlowe followed everyone to the basement and stuck his snout in the box, curious.

"Aw, you rescued my stuff," Charlie said. He was touched.

He picked up an audio cassette of Karen Carpenter songs. I remember Charlie had a soft spot for her. It was called *Karen Sings the Blues*, and it must have been from his side, because I don't think she recorded it in this world. Charlie got wistful as he read the song titles.

"'*My Man*,' originally sung by Billie Holiday. '*House of the Rising Sun*.' She does an awesome version of that. '*Little Red Rooster*.'"

"It was so sad when she died," Tim said.

Charlie blinked and almost dropped the cassette. "She died? When?" He was heartbroken.

"Yeah, it was in—"

"Eureka!" I shouted. My hand shot in the air gripping a fistful of Charlie's Polaroid photos from 1995.

I quickly handed them to Tim. The creature in the photos was a bit faded, but clear enough. Charlie and I watched Tim intently, hopefully, as he peered at one picture, then another, then another.

"This is what my nightmares were about," I said. "And now there are more."

After a moment, Tim looked up. First he addressed Charlie.

"So you haven't been in Australia all this time, tossin' shrimp on the barbie?"

"Nope. Living in my dimension, working in a lab."

Tim turned to me. His eyes were steady, his expression resolute. "I'm going to need my own shot of tequila," he said. "Then we can swing by my office on the way for some pharmaceutical backup."

I was overwhelmed with love for this man, but right now we had a world to save. I grabbed a baseball bat sticking out of another box. Charlie pulled out one of my snow skis. He considered Marlowe, still nosing around in everything.

"Does your dog bark?" he asked.

As we pulled up and parked in the same spot past Muck

Creek Bridge, the sun was at its midpoint in the sky. Charlie said that was good for keeping everything in our sights. There was going to be a lot of activity, he said. The ski was sticking out the window, and Charlie was squashed in back with equipment and a wiggly dog.

Because he had the longest arms, I made Charlie take some selfies. We were quite a group. Tim had stuffed his pockets with hypos of Novocain, leaving a free hand to hold Marlowe's leash. I had my baseball bat and two 10-pound tanks of nitrous oxide. Charlie had his phone and my ski. We thought between the three of us and the barking dog, it should be enough to scare the creatures into the portal.

Silent and grim, we made our way through the tall grass. I just kept thinking if I lost Tim, I'd never forgive myself. But we'd always been good at having each other's backs. He was peering ahead uncertainly, and I was curious to see what he'd do when he saw the creatures.

I didn't have long to wait. They had clumped together a bit, crouched near the maple tree. What were they thinking, I wondered. Did they think at all, or was everything just instinct? Two of them straightened to full height on our approach. We stopped a few yards away.

"Holy cow," Tim murmured. "They're grosser in person."

Charlie was counting. "...three, four, five. Where's number six?"

"Maybe back in the portal?" I offered hopefully.

"We can't depend on that." Charlie pulled out his phone and pushed buttons. "Tim, do you see the portal? That dark anomaly near the ground?"

Tim squinted toward the grass close by and then nodded. "Got it."

"Good. Lauren, we'll angle around from each side and get behind them, then drive them to the portal. Tim, you stay here with the dog so they don't run past it."

"Wait," Tim said.

I expected Tim to say he was bailing. I was the athlete in the marriage—skiing, running, hiking. Tim liked to walk the dog, but otherwise he was more of a couch-and-gamer.

But Tim only handed Charlie and me some hypos and took one of the nitrous oxide canisters. He gave me a quick kiss and smiled. "Okay."

That was when Marlowe noticed the creatures and all hell broke loose.

Barking, Marlowe bolted for the creatures, almost yanking Tim off his feet. Three of the things scattered, grunting in panic. The two others shuffled menacingly at Marlowe and Tim.

Charlie and I switched directions and went for those two creatures. Charlie raised his phone, but the cacophonous music was drowned out by Marlowe's barks. It didn't matter anyway, because the creature nearest Charlie reached rubbery fingers and swiped the phone from Charlie's hand. It fell to the ground, buried in the tall grass, still playing music. Charlie took a swing with the ski, but the creature dodged out of the way.

I swung my bat at the creature nearest to me, connected with its back, and sent it sprawling. Then Charlie was on it, whacking it with the ski. I turned to see the other creature running at Tim, but he was ready, Marlowe's leash wound around one arm. The dog stood his ground, barking ferociously. In Tim's other arm was the canister; he aimed, turned the spigot, and shot nitrous oxide full in the face of the creature as it got to him.

The creature staggered back, its orange eyes going almost black, then back to orange. It shuddered. It staggered some more. I came at it with the bat and knocked it to the ground. I raised the bat, but then I stopped. Its eyes had closed. Was it dead? I remembered what Charlie had said about murder. I turned to see him give his creature's legs a few shots of Novocain and then drag it toward the portal, so I did the same, hypoing, then grabbing mine's rubbery legs and following Charlie. It felt like dragging a bag of cement.

Charlie and I looked at each other, gasping but relieved. Bullets might not faze these things, but apparently drugs worked like gangbusters.

Tim meanwhile let Marlowe drag him toward another creature that had pinned itself against the maple tree, shivering, clearly terrified. Tim took Marlowe's collar and ordered him to heel. For once, the dog obeyed and stood whining.

I heard Tim say, "Sorry," and then he blasted the creature in the face with nitrous oxide.

Charlie and I gave its legs some shots of Novocain and dragged it to the portal. Midway, it awoke, its legs flopping around, already numbed, as it attempted to stand. We shoved it inside the portal.

Charlie said, "That's three."

The two that had scattered earlier had come back and were poking at Charlie's cell phone in the grass. Were they attracted by the music or desperately trying to turn it off? With the three of us surrounding them and Marlowe encouraged to bark again, we succeeded in driving the two creatures to the portal. They seemed relieved to crawl back in, though the second one turned to give us a long, baleful glare before disappearing inside. I had the feeling it was memorizing our faces.

Tim, Charlie, and I paused near the portal to catch our breath. Charlie turned off the music, putting the pasture into blissful quiet. We were sweaty and disheveled. Tim gave Marlowe some dog treats from his pocket. After a few minutes, we all started to smile.

"Don't relax yet," Charlie said. Though he was grinning the most.

We joined Charlie on a reconnaissance of the pasture for more creatures. Tim and I took turns walking with Marlowe as he sniffed around. We even looked under Muck

Creek Bridge itself. Charlie seemed ready to give the all-clear.

Tim kept gazing thoughtfully at the portal.

"These creatures," he said, "they're intelligent."

Charlie picked up on what he was saying. "Very. And that's my next assignment. Studying them, forging some kind of communication if we can. From our end. Maybe someday from yours."

We stood a while longer, talking about the old days. We knew Charlie's time with us was coming to a close. Charlie pushed some buttons on his cell phone device and showed us.

"Once I set the timer, I'll only have a few seconds to get through the portal before it closes for the next thirty years."

"Wouldn't be so bad if you stayed," I said.

Charlie grinned. "I wish you could meet my wife."

I was trying not to cry. Tim was in the same boat.

"What about the other creatures down there?" I asked. "Will they attack you?"

"I'll be okay," Charlie insisted. "Just a short hop to my own world. You'll hear from me again, I swear."

Tim and I said we'd keep an eye on the old sheep farm, and the town in general, in case some creatures had wandered away. We knew we could handle things. Charlie said with a laugh he had no doubts we could.

We all hugged a long time. Charlie ruffled Marlowe's

ears. Then he pushed some final buttons. Crouched at the portal, he turned to me and said with a grin, "Remember breakfast at Fitch's."

The sixth creature came out of the tall grass from full crouch to maximum attack. It went for Marlowe, maybe thinking the dog was the least threat. Before we could react, it picked up Marlowe and swung him, then threw him. Tim shouted and lunged at the thing bare-handed. As the dog tumbled to a landing some feet away, Tim yanked the creature's arm. It whirled back and knocked Tim tumbling in the other direction.

I hit it with the bat so hard wood splintered and flew. The creature grabbed my throat with its clawed hand and yanked me to it. We were eye to eye. Its orange orbs felt hot on my face. They were so cavernous I could see the multiverse inside them.

Then there was a loud thunk as Charlie brought a metal canister down on the creature's head. It let go of me, buckled, and hit the ground. I fell, choking, and crawled to Tim.

But the creature was up again. If they had adrenaline, this one was pumped. Charlie aimed the sprayer, but no nitrous oxide came out; it was jammed or empty. Charlie and the creature grabbed each other in a bizarre scuffling dance.

Charlie's phone device dropped to the tall grass.

"Charlie!" I shouted, struggling to my feet.

Fleshy, gray-green fingers reached up from the portal, then rubbery arms—another creature coming out.

Charlie glanced at me, then at the portal. I knew what he was thinking. Only seconds.

I staggered toward him, crouching to leap for his phone. Maybe I could stop the timer.

In a split second, Charlie wrapped the creature in one of his famous bear hugs and launched them both sideways at the portal opening.

The emerging creature disappeared under the two bodies smashing through the portal. The last I saw of Charlie was his khaki pants cuff and sneaker slipping into the opening. Then he and the creatures were gone.

I found Charlie's phone in the tall grass. Something like a timer display said 0:00:00. The portal suddenly grew and shimmered more strongly, which made me worried. Then it gradually shrank and faded, shrank more and faded more. Then it was gone. I ran my hands over the spot, and it was just dry, rustly grass.

Tim was examining Marlowe, who seemed to have the wind knocked out of him but otherwise appeared okay. He licked our hands to reassure us.

I showed Tim Charlie's phone.

"Doesn't he need it to get back?" he asked.

"I don't know." I stared at where the portal had been. "Do you…think he'll make it?"

Tim reached for my hand and squeezed it.

Things went pretty much back to normal then, and no more nightmares. Tim went back to filling cavities, and I went back to grading English papers. Marlowe got a good exam at the vet and checked out. We took him with us on our patrols most evenings.

One night a week or two later I heard Charlie's phone device beep. I always kept it close, but I never expected it to work again. I hurried to look at the screen.

There were two photos. The first was of Charlie standing next to Karen Carpenter, petite, gray-haired, and smiling, obviously still alive in his world and going strong. I chuckled.

The second photo was also of Charlie standing next to a woman. This time it was Mrs. Valerie Barton of gardening fame—of course his side's version. Charlie had found Valerie in his world and married her. They held out their hands to show their rings, and she was smiling as happily as he was.

Below, Charlie had messaged: "She's even more beautiful in my world."

When Tim came home from work, I showed him the photos.

"Good old Charlie," he said. Then he said he also had news.

"One of my patients today told me there was a weird animal going through her trash cans last night. Like a hairless coyote or something. When she turned on the porch light, it grunted and ran away, she said."

Tim's expression was a mix of apprehension and excitement—mostly excitement. I waited for my usual reaction of gut fear. But it never came.

"Should we suit up?" Tim asked. "I have more nitrous in the car."

I smiled and put Charlie's phone device in my pocket. "I'll grab Marlowe."

SOJOURN

As she trudged across the rocky sand, shivering, she stared at the one dim star in the sky and wondered how the inhabitants of this soggy planet could see anything. Her gasps were harsh and wet. She was breathing water.

Lost, drowning, she knew she wouldn't make the rendezvous. Her companions would leave without her, abandon her in this cold, sodden, desolate place.

Movement to her right startled her, and she stumbled, then caught herself. A curious feathered creature, brown and mottled, struggled in the sand, one wing flapping. Its other wing appeared broken. Its head was bowed. A brown serpent chased the feathered creature, triangular head reaching, mouth agape and full of fangs. A whirl of kicked-up dust enveloped them.

Ignoring the gurgle in her throat, she stopped to watch. The serpent was patient but determined, following the feathered creature in circles, dodging its powerful wing as it thrashed. She thought the serpent wasn't cruel, just hungry. But she felt for the feathered creature as it fought for its life.

She coughed, doubled over, staggered to one side. She remained hunched and shaky until her gasps subsided. She didn't have much time. Her companions would wait only until the deadline. They might search for her if they felt inclined, but it wasn't part of protocol.

The feathered creature now lay sideways, panting, clawed feet splayed, beak open, eyes glazed and bright. It had been struggling for a long time. She could almost feel its utter exhaustion and hopelessness. The serpent rested too, expectant, in the shade of a great boulder. Neither seemed to notice her.

She and her companions weren't to interfere in the actions of this planet's inhabitants. But she couldn't watch this, and she couldn't walk away.

Wary, she moved toward the serpent. It saw her and spun into an angry coil, tail rattling, forked tongue darting. She stooped, almost fell, but straightened again and in her fist was a rock.

She raised her arm and threw. A dull thunk as the rock landed on the serpent. It jumped, struck out at air, and recoiled. She kicked the ground with her boot. The serpent struck again, but she pelted it with handfuls of sand. Finally it yielded, slithering off to find easier prey. Soon it was out of sight amid brush and spiked plants.

She gave a rheumy cough. The feathered creature didn't move. Peering closer, she saw the reason for its trouble: its head and one wing were entangled in a flat, opaque, flexible apparatus with six rings. She had no idea its purpose, but realized it was a death trap for anything caught in it.

She kneeled carefully next to the feathered creature, saw its sharp eyes widen in panic. She reached gentle hands to the milky yoke of rings. They were strong. But she found if she pulled, the material stretched, widened. And finally, with the last of her strength, she broke two rings apart.

The creature didn't hesitate. Free, its head snapped up, both wings arced, opened—she felt the gust of them on her face, heard the flapping—and the feathered brown body rose into the air. Nothing like this magnificent being that owned the sky existed on her planet. Her heart rose and flew with it, her eyes squinting as they followed it away on the horizon.

Then she lay gratefully on the sand near a tall, thorny plant, amid the buzz of insects and meager heat from the dim star. The day continued around her.

Her companions would search for her—she believed that. They'd find her. They'd be there soon.

FLY

Nichols is yelling and waving his arms about something when Brenner brings Luke in for their last meal before they head out.

"Enough with the Tourette's, Nichols," Brenner says. "Just serve the eggs."

"Look!" Nichols jabs a finger toward the window. "It's space! It's space, and we still can't get away from the damn things!"

"Actually, it's a planet," Luke jokes. But Brenner shoots him a frown, so he shuts up.

They notice the fly repeatedly butt up against the station's one window, hear the high whining buzz. Its buckshot body reflects blue-green in the sunlight. They have a stowaway.

"They're in the ship, all the way here. They get on the food. And now they're in the station. Where the hell do they come from?" Nichols demands, waving the spatula.

Luke wolfs four helpings of eggs and toast and bacon and coffee. The eggs are powdered, the toast flat, the bacon dry, the coffee stale—but it's the most delicious meal Luke has eaten in months. Nichols just keeps making more, and eventually he forgets about the fly, and Luke listens to him and Brenner talk about home and how they got all the way out here.

Nichols had been a pilot in the war and afterwards wanted to travel. He'd flown freight and passengers for years. "And saw more godforsaken corners of the galaxy than anyone should," he adds with a chuckle. "But it's all good."

Brenner just went where the company told him, scouting planets to find those with the right conditions. He points out the window at the yellowish sky.

"This is what they tend to pick. Uninhabited, of course. Some atmosphere. This one's better than most because of the stable temps. Hot but not too hot. You'll do all right."

"I went to school to be a pilot," Luke says.

"Oh, get your license?" Nichols asks.

"No," Luke says. "I didn't finish."

A pause. Brenner finally says, "Look where we all ended up."

Luke packs his handful of clothes, slips on his granddad's class ring, and he's set to go. He got the ring at the old man's deathbed twenty-eight years before. It's all Luke has left of him, of any of his family. The stone, a blue zircon he remembers, fell out years ago. But the gold band has held up pretty good.

The three men put on soft suits, gloves, and helmets for the trip out. Nichols drives, Brenner beside him. Luke is in back, and after a few miles they cover his helmet so he can't see where he's going.

The soft suit feels cool, the air circulating well. The helmet is hot, though, and constrictive, and the cover makes him claustrophobic. Luke doesn't know how long they drive over rocky dirt, sometimes swooping up and down through hilly areas, sometimes changing course or even doubling back. He guesses about four hours, but he can't get a feel for time with the sensory deprivation.

They finally stop, and Brenner removes the cover from Luke's helmet.

"Last stop," Luke murmurs.

They all get out. The planet's sun is bright. The wind is hard enough to make Luke sway before he catches himself.

Brenner asks him, "Want me to send a message to anyone back home?"

Luke shakes his head. "There's no one."

Brenner hands Luke a pack. "That's six liters of water. Should be enough to get you there if you drink sparingly. The facility is ninety-four miles due east." Brenner taps the tracker module on the wrist of Luke's soft suit. "Stay in a straight line and follow the coordinates. You'll find it."

"Food?"

"No food."

"It could be three days."

"More like four, 'cause you'll be weaker and slower toward the end," Nichols says.

Brenner gives Luke a steady gaze. "No food."

Luke considers the eastern horizon. Nothing but dirt

and rock, some flat, some hilly, some mountainous. No plant life. No life at all.

"Most make it, we hear," Nichols says.

"Is there really a prison there? Or am I just wandering in the desert until I die?"

"That's part of it," Brenner says flatly. "You don't know for sure."

"Some of 'em turn around and try to follow us back," Nichols says. "The wind erases the tire tracks fast, so they really are just wandering. And to a dead end. Follow your tracker. Go east."

"Thanks for the eggs," Luke says.

It takes everything he has, but Luke doesn't turn around, not even when he hears the truck head back the way they came. Its rumble fades behind him, and soon it's gone. As he starts going east, all he hears is the wind and his boots plodding on the dirt.

The mountains and foothills are a dull orange, and so is the dirt and rock that covers it. They take him back to when he lived in southern California. At least there was scrub and cactus and some trees there, but not here.

Still, it comforts him. He pretends he's walking Indian Canyon or the trails outside of Palm Springs, saying good morning to other hikers and their little dogs. Occasionally there would be a plastic baggy of scooped poop on the side of the trail, and it would be there days later, because the dog owner would have forgotten to pick it up. And at the height of hiking season there'd be several baggies, which always made Luke think of the dead bodies of hikers littered along the trail to the top of Everest.

He trudges along, keeps his pace steady. And then, a high, whiny buzz in his helmet. At first he thinks the wind is playing tricks on his ears. Then he sees the dark bullet shape in his peripheral vision.

A fly, or maybe the same fly from that morning, has hitched a ride somewhere in his soft suit and made its way to his helmet.

It lands on his cheek. He flinches, hits the flat of his palm hard on the faceplate. The fly takes off fast, whizzing around Luke's head in angry ellipses punctuated by its frantic whine-buzz.

Luke removes his helmet, the pneumatic seal unhitching with a whoosh. The fly swoops up, is waylaid sideways by the wind, then corrects its course and flies off, seemingly as happy to be free as Luke is to be rid of it.

What did Nichols say? "Can't get away from 'em," Luke murmurs, and laughs.

He takes tentative sips of air. It tastes thin and chalky and old, like the inside of an empty room. He experiments with deeper breaths as he walks. Too deep and he inhales the orange dust carried in the wind, so shallow is better. He finds if he takes some hits off the air intake tube every few minutes, it's doable.

The sun is hot on his head without the helmet's

protection, though, so he digs into his pack, finds a T-shirt, and wraps it into a sort of turban. It's comforting and soaks up his sweat.

And he walks, helmet swinging in his hand.

The wind makes a sound, which is why he doesn't notice at first when the fly is back. But there's its tiny shadow looping around the orange dirt at his feet, the high-pitched whiny hum around his head. The fly lands on Luke's neck. He brushes at it, causing it to swoop up and circle him. Soon it lands on him again. He keeps swatting at it.

"Want to feast on my corpse? Then lay eggs and hatch a new colony of vermin? I don't think so."

Every time he feels the tickling, he swats at the fly. Finally it gets the hint and buzzes away against the wind. Luke watches it disappear into the yellow horizon before he continues onward.

The sun is relentless, but the helmet is too stifling to wear, so Luke drinks some water instead, careful to take just a few sips. This has to last—the equivalent of three days on Earth, maybe four. And if the prison is all a lie, maybe for many days.

The sun beats down. He walks. The mountains on the horizon never seem to get any closer. After eight hours and almost 26 miles—he keeps track on the module—he comes to an area of boulders as big as cars, some as big as houses. His granddad's ring slips down his sweaty finger, but he catches it before it can fall off. He sits in the shade to rest.

A day on this planet lasts almost an Earth month, so he knows there will be no nightfall, no real relief from the heat and glare. This will have to do. Soon his eyes droop.

He hears, as he always does, the click of the detonator and a second later the explosion. When he opens his eyes, he's disoriented, checks his tracker module to see two hours have passed. His lungs feel like they're being squeezed, and he quickly finds the air intake and huffs oxygen.

Getting to his feet, he thinks he hears the fly. But no, it's the wind making that whine. He starts walking, taking precious sips of water.

He's glad he ate so much breakfast; otherwise, he'd be hungrier.

He negotiates hilly areas, nothing too steep, and then a flat expanse of pockmarked dirt and dusty horizon. He checks his module to see another three hours have gone by.

And where is the fly? Did it discover other company on this godforsaken rock? Maybe it found its way back to the station and nonchalantly buzzed inside when Nichols opened the door for a smoke. Maybe it's lapping reconstituted maple syrup off the kitchen counter right now. Or maybe it's miles ahead at the prison, lapping sweat off the neck of another poor bastard like himself.

Ten hours later, when his eyes hurt from the relentless glare and he's walked only four more hours and then slept or sat the rest of the time, that breakfast seems like years ago. Forty-six miles, so he's almost halfway. But it's hot, he's tired, and he knows he needs to pace himself even as he wastes precious time. The odds he'll even make it are against him. He knows that too.

An hour later he stares up the side of a steep, rocky foothill. Brenner told him to follow the coordinates. Too easy to lose your way. So he sips some water and then starts climbing. No food, but there will be food when he gets there. And people to let him in. If it even exists. If it isn't a lie, like all the other lies in his life. All the times they said they'd be there and they weren't.

Back on level ground four hours and eight miles later, he decides if the fly was here, he'd eat it. One satisfying crunch. And a gulp of water to wash it down.

Exhausted, he sits and rests. And sleeps. When he hears the detonator click and a second later the explosion, he jolts awake. He looks east and almost doesn't get to his feet. But he does.

Has the fly discovered food somewhere out there in the orange rock and dirt? Should he try to find it? Something edible to a fly would probably be edible to a human. How much DNA did they share? Sixty percent, that's what he heard somewhere, probably in prison before. Sixty percent.

Three more hours, and he veers left. The fly went this way, right? No, that was long ago. He corrects his course. Two more hours, and he goes left again, then forces himself back on track. Now he's delirious? Sun mad? Going off course to see if the fly found food—he's off his nut. If he's this bad already, what's going to happen in the next several hours? He has to keep it together.

He checks his tracker module. Sixty-four miles. He checks his water. How does he have just two liters left?

He realizes somewhere along the way he dropped his helmet. Not that he was using it, but he turns, looking. He trips, then catches himself. Some rocks shift, and he starts to slide, boots scuffing. It's only a short hill, but he stumbles to one knee and skids down. He shouts as agony arrows through his kneecap.

For a moment he catches his breath, then tries to get up. No dice.

Nearby are more large boulders giving off meager shade. He crawls back up the hill and sits heavily against them and wipes the sweat off his crusty face. He holds his knee and rocks and gasps at the pain.

He could have been a pilot and seen all the corners of the galaxy, too, just like Nichols, if he'd finished the program. But he'd had to quit and get a job. He'd always meant to go back. But other people had spouses or relatives to help them with the bills. He didn't have anybody.

And that story about the prison? Just ninety-four miles east, just follow the tracker. Right. If he didn't trip here, he would have soon tripped over the carcasses of the other prisoners before him they fed that lie to, all trying to get there, all hoping someone was waiting to let them in. Of course there's no prison. This is the punishment.

    He knows his odds have tanked. He's already dead. It just won't be official until the water runs out.

    He slouches, his back to the rock, and closes his eyes against the glare of the sun.

    When he hears the click of the detonator and then the explosion, he realizes he's fallen asleep again. He feels the detonator still in his hand, watches a hundred people on fire stumble and fall and become blackened bodies, hears a high-pitched whine-buzz.

    Luke starts awake at the tickle on the back of his neck. His hand comes up to swat, but instead he opens his eyes and lowers his hand. It's drinking. It's just thirsty after all. Like he is.

    He reaches carefully down for his tracker module. The fly stays put on his neck. He doesn't even feel it now, only sees in the dirt its tiny pebble shadow blended with his. He holds up the tracker screen angled against the sun, catches a wobbly reflection of the fly as it grooms itself, its bulbous red eyes cocked at the sky.

    The ambient noise is gone, the air clearer. The wind has died to almost nothing. Luke realizes the wind has done its work, though, as he sucks at his air intake tube. Clogged with dust. He draws harder and gets a thin feed.

    Luke savors the last few sips of his water. Then, careful not to make sudden movements that would disturb the fly, he struggles to one foot. The fly stays. Twelve hours of wasted time, but resting did him good. He puts weight on his bad leg, knows the knee is swollen and hard under his suit. He feels a dull but doable pain. Time to get moving, and at first it's in clumsy jerks, but soon he eases into a steady limp.

The fly, his faithful stowaway, stays put. Thirty miles to go. The sun, now more intense in the clearer atmosphere, beats in Luke's eyes. Somewhere he lost his T-shirt turban, and he worries the river of sweat on his neck might be too much. But the fly hangs on, steadfast, its shadow a sturdy lump. One crunch, a gulp of water, but then where would he be? Still hungry and alone.

Luke hobbles along. He makes his mind blank, thinking only of his forward motion and the fly on his neck. His leg is numb below his engorged knee. His mouth is raw and dry. His chest is a tight spring. When his sweat starts to plop and splatter in the orange dirt, though, he gets uneasy. It's liquid. It should be conserved.

He pauses to check his tracker: almost 83 miles. Eleven more to go before he can rest and eat. At this pace, a day's walk. Normally much less, but for him a day.

The top of his head burns, making him dizzy. He needs to cover it. But as he reaches for his pack, the commotion disturbs the fly. It rises into the air, and he freezes. It makes a jerky, uneven circle, lands again on Luke's neck. He realizes the fly is as weak as he is.

Bigger drops of sweat splatter down. He can't stand it,

stumbles to the dirt and puts his lips to the wetness. The fly whirs upward, struggling. Luke turns, cries out as the tiny body drops to the ground. It thrashes in a frantic, whining circle. Luke reaches a shaking hand but then draws back. The fly tries to walk, falls over, totters to its feet. It falls to its back. Its legs twitch.

Luke sprawls lower and lays his cheek on the ground, eye to fly. It twitches and buzzes, is still, twitches and buzzes again. Luke's tight chest heaves. His ragged breaths puff on the orange dirt.

"I didn't mean it," he whispers. "I didn't mean it." It's all he can manage. He hopes the fly sees a thousand images of him looking back at it. That would be comforting—having a thousand friends with you when you go.

For several minutes, the world is only dust and sun and the fading struggles of the fly. Even when it's finally quiet, Luke doesn't get up, but obsessively checks his tracker module. An hour passes with no movement, no twitch. Only then does Luke slide another T-shirt from his pack and wrap it around his sweaty head.

He scoops a slow handful of orange dirt, then another. He carefully cups the fly in his palm. It shimmers blue green as Luke places it in the hole he's made. After a moment, Luke slips off his granddad's ring and snugs it next to the fly. He doesn't have any words, but he bows his head. He thinks of all the places the fly has been in its short life. He covers the grave with dirt and tamps it so the wind doesn't kick it up.

Wiping sweat from his face, Luke gets to weary feet, sways a moment. He takes a shallow, dusty hit of oxygen. A day's walk, that's all. A day. He limps off, his bloodshot gaze on the yellow horizon.

FALLEN

I caught him in my arms as the others ran for safety in the shelters. The fires began to die around us. I sat on the ground and held him while the sliver rays took their inevitable toll. An agonizing way to go, the rays. They moved fast and deadly through your insides—too fast and too many to remove or repair.

"Did it...work?" He could barely rasp out the words.

"Yes, you did it." I swiped tears from my eyes so he wouldn't see them. "Everyone made it."

He nodded, relieved. The snow fell in light, cold whispers that melted to nothing. It made promises we all needed to believe: more seasons, more time.

"Remember—" he started, and then he was racked with coughing.

I grasped his hand. Mine shook badly. "Yes?"

"Remember our drive...in the mountains?"

I nodded. It had been last fall, a warm day with only the hint of chill. We'd met the month before, new recruits unsure of how bad the invasion would become.

On a day leave, our last, we'd changed into civilian clothes, run through the rain to his solar truck, then driven east toward the snowcapped mountains. Only an hour from the city, the highway had risen, the towns had become smaller, and the rain had stopped.

We'd seen a bald eagle high in a fir tree, and when we'd driven past, it had flown up, great, dark wings arching and white head dipping as it glided over the nearby river.

"Wouldn't it be great to move up here," he'd said. "See, this is something real, something you can touch. There's an eagle. There's the river. There are mountains. Concrete things, beautiful things. Not like death. That's a concept. You can't see it or touch it. It only becomes real in the absence of something."

He hadn't talked about it before—the impending war and what it might cost us. Driving on, he'd looked steadily at the road and become silent. I'd taken his hand and he'd squeezed mine back, and we'd found a motel, and when we had undressed and come together, his body had been warm and relaxed and strong.

"This is real," he'd said, our eyes locked, his hand on my face.

By that evening when we'd returned to the barracks, our orders were waiting for us.

"I remember," I said softly now. I smiled and put my forehead against his cheek. So many things to say, and now they'd be lost. "I remember."

I felt his face contract. A smile of love, I hoped, and not a grimace of pain from the sliver rays. I pulled away to look. It was neither—a twist of his mouth. Regret. Sorrow.

"Sorry for...being stupid," he said.

"No, don't. You saved—"

"We should've had a lifetime."

He coughed again, hard, blood at his lips. It would happen now. I would lose him.

I held his face and willed my hands to be steady. In the moment my eyes met his, we lived a thousand years. Ten thousand. Still not enough, but they would have to do.

"I'm here," I said. "I won't let go."

I felt his warm skin. The rough sleeve of his uniform. The ground beneath us, safe for now. These were real, concrete things. You could touch them. Goodbye was a concept. It only became real in the absence of something. Of someone.

He closed his eyes. I sat with him. Bombs went off in the distance, but I heard only the whispers of the falling snow.

THE NYX EFFECT

Funny how when you throw people together and shake them up, they're pulled into a sort of doomed syzygy of events they can't control. I later thought about that a lot, how what happened seemed inevitable, like riding a falling star knowing at some point it has to burn up in the atmosphere.

We were five intrepid writers who met every week at Beeno's Espresso to critique each others' work. I was comfortable talking about writing in a group setting, but I admit I showed a reluctance, though not what my ex-wife called "standoffish poopyness," to fully participate in anything more personal.

Until, a year into my stint with the group, Maddie one night revealed a recurring nightmare she'd started having as a child, and it struck something in me that finally squirmed its way out.

As the five of us would arrive at Beeno's and buy our various caffeine fixes and sit around the table, we'd briefly touch on our weeks, our jobs, our families, small talk to pass the time until everyone was settled. Inevitably the subjects grew deeper, and soon every week we mostly talked about our dreams and how they might relate to our writing.

Since college I'd been working sporadically on a series of Tolkienesque novels while teaching high school English. Maddie wrote what we all wanted to dismiss as chick-lit, but only because we were jealous. Her stories were actually astute, humorous narratives of real life. She'd sold a couple to regional magazines, the only one of our group to publish.

Maddie was going through a difficult time with her current boyfriend, a control freak, and to me her latest dream was an obvious metaphor for her stifling relationship. "I was sitting in a room," she was saying, her hands with their trim nails arcing in the air to help create a visual, "and it was bare except for the chair I was in, a metal folding chair. And the paint was peeling off the walls, and there were no windows, and no fresh air. I could barely breathe."

"So what happened?" Andrew asked. A video-game nerd, Andrew wrote and illustrated clumsy graphic novels. I was probably a snob, but I imagined Andrew's dreams were earnest ones of killing terrorists or dragons while half-dressed Princess Leia look-alikes waited breathlessly to reward him.

"Hmm." Maddie crinkled her nose in thought. "I kept trying to stand up, to get out of the chair, but it was like something was holding me down. And when I finally could stand, I just wandered around the room looking for a way out."

"Well, that's not obvious or anything," I blurted. I couldn't stay silent anymore.

All eyes swiveled my way in surprise—I so rarely gave an opinion. Jesse arched a derisive brow as if in challenge. I knew he had a crush on Maddie.

The newest member of the group, Jesse was my age, 33, and wrote adventure novels with a little Nietzschean philosophy thrown in. His dreams involved lots of scaling of high mountains or crossing of dense jungles. So did his stories, and I had to admit they were good.

"It's your relationship." I ignored Jesse's glower and forged ahead. "Or your relationships plural, I guess. When you feel stressed or unsure. The room is you, sort of, er, or your frame of mind. How you deal with the room and the chair is how you feel about what's troubling you in your waking life. In this case, you're feeling smothered and trapped in your relationship, and your dream is manifesting that feeling."

I wasn't sure where all this was coming from, this sudden pseudo-Freudian blabber spewing from my mouth, but it sounded right to me. And from the appreciative look Maddie gave me, I was on target. It gave me a rush of confidence I hadn't had since before my marriage went sour.

"Thanks, Ned," Maddie said softly. Her eyes held mine. "That helped."

"So, Mr. Psychology," Walter's tone was teasing, "we've yet to hear a dream from you. And don't say you don't dream, because everybody dreams." At 72, 'the codger,' as we lovingly called Walter, usually described dreams about his family or his job at a bank, and he wrote about them as well.

With a glance at Maddie for reassurance, I nodded, took a deep breath, and jumped in. "Fair enough. In keeping with tonight's theme, I'll tell you about a recurring dream I've had since I was young."

I had to give a bit of background first. When I was a kid, the kid who lived across the street had everything I didn't. Whenever he got a new bike, I'd look at my old rusty one and seethe. If he could jump off his garage roof five times, I jumped off mine ten times, secretly, proving I could do it better. So when the kid's dog had six puppies, I put my two pet rats together in the same cage my dad had built in the garage, and pretty soon they had babies. And then the babies grew up and had babies. After a few months, I had two dozen pet rats living in the same cage.

I didn't know what to do, but I let it continue. I always gave them food and water, but there were too many living creatures in a small space. They would fight. They would make lots of noise. Then the mom rats killed some of their babies. That's when my parents finally stepped in and I had to take them all to the pet store and give them away, even my favorite rat, Elliott, who had a pretty black hooded pattern on his back and who would sit on my shoulder and let me hand-feed him.

"That summer afterward I had nightmares about the rats," I said. Fighting each other, eating each other, stuck in their cramped little cage. But the worst one, the recurring dream, was always the same. It was a typical morning, and I went barefoot to the garage to feed the rats. But this morning the cage was filled with dozens and dozens of half-eaten little bodies, blood everywhere, and the door to the cage was open. I frantically searched for Elliott, hoping he'd survived, but I couldn't see him. Was Elliott dead, now nothing but remains decomposing and buried in the cage floor's bloody cedar shavings?

A noise in the corner of the garage, like something shifting, made me turn. A beast, a thing with yellow fangs that looked like Elliott but was as big as a St. Bernard, crouched in front of me, its eyes blazing with rage. I had no time to scream, no room to run. The monster Elliott lunged, seized my torso in its jaws, shook me like a doll, and then ate me. In my dream it didn't hurt, but I always abruptly woke with a peculiar numbness in my arms and legs.

When I was finished telling my dream, Jesse gave a dismissive shrug.

Andrew, though, had been listening, rapt, his expression grave. "Dude," he said quietly. "Did you know that if you die in your dreams, you die in real life? But it sounds like you do it all the time, and you don't die." So far Andrew, like I until that night, had refrained from talking about his dreams.

"It's a strange feeling, though," I admitted.

"It's so, I don't know…sweet. And definitely sad."

Maddie's voice was gentle. "You feel this obsession, obsession that eats you alive. When was the last time you had the dream?"

I tried to make light of it. "Well, less and less since my divorce," I answered. The joke didn't land, but I realized I wasn't as uncomfortable as I thought I'd be hearing Maddie sort of bare my soul.

Jesse downed his coffee and crumpled the paper cup in his fist. "I got that beat," he said. I knew I'd heard that phrase before and realized Jesse was mimicking Richard Dreyfuss. "I got that beat," he said again and grinned, looking at all of us in turn. "One time when I was a kid, I watched *Jaws* like five times in a row. Then for weeks I had nightmares of getting attacked by sharks. In one, I was eaten by a Great White, and while I was inside its mouth, I saw the teeth closing," Jesse splayed his fingers, one hand above the other, making them come together, "and closing," his fingers joined, "and then…" he paused for dramatic effect, "…all was darkness."

Andrew was impressed. "Man. You died too."

"Yep," Jesse said, and he smiled at me in triumph. He was competitive from the beginning, always bringing in more pages of manuscript than anyone else, entering writing contest after writing contest, becoming morose but even more determined when he didn't win. And early on, he seemed to notice my interest in Maddie and made it a point to chat with her before the meetings started.

The next week I walked into the meeting a few minutes late while Maddie was in the middle of her latest dream:

"...And then the whole sky became thick, like a haze," she was saying. "Well, more like an ooze. It was oozing muddy, yogurty stuff all over everything, turning it reddish brown. It was falling on the cars, the stores. The street. Everywhere."

"Maybe it's your new story," Andrew suggested. "Like you think it's covered in rust or something. You do keep saying it's not coming together."

"Maybe," Maddie agreed. She looked thoughtful. "Oh, and I was looking up at it, you know? My face was tilted up, and some of it plopped onto my face." She crinkled her nose. "God, it sounds like semen." Her tone was serious until she noticed the rest of us staring, amused. "Oops, did I say that out loud?" She started to giggle.

Walter, the codger, grinned and ran a hand through his full head of white hair. "Hey, just because at my age it takes a while to get it cranked up, don't mean what comes out is rusty."

Andrew blushed. The rest of us burst into laughter. Maddie collapsed in her chair in a fit of giggles. I loved that about her, how she couldn't stop if something struck her funny, how she'd become just weak with laughter.

After our meeting ended, Maddie and I stayed at the table finishing our coffees. She asked if I would share a piece of pie with her, and I said I would. Jesse lingered a minute, pretending to make some notes on his manuscript pages, but he could tell he was treading in third-wheel territory and eventually said goodnight. I wonder if that was the deciding moment in what happened between Jesse and me after that.

As we finished our pie, Maddie and I talked about writing, jobs, favorite movies—normal group-meeting stuff. But we both found ourselves smiling more. And our goodnight hug felt charged with possibilities.

Andrew's alien invasion came during the next week's meeting.

When I sat down with my coffee and greeted the group, I noticed with dismay that Maddie hadn't arrived yet. I'd thought about her the whole week, wanting to call her but wondering if she'd think it was too weird. As far as I knew, she still had the boyfriend.

Andrew was almost bouncing in his chair, alternating between excitement and nervousness. We were critiquing his first non-illustrated piece, an adventure story that he said he hoped Jesse, especially, would like, as it was right up Jesse's alley.

I only half listened as Andrew spoke, because just then Maddie came in the door and went to the counter to order her usual macchiato. She looked tired and distracted. I secretly, guiltily hoped all was not well in boyfriend land.

Jesse pushed back his chair and wandered over to the counter behind her. I shifted uncomfortably, watching.

Jesse wasn't getting anything himself but seemed to be offering to buy Maddie her coffee. But she shook her head, barely looking at him, hunching her shoulders. I couldn't help but be pleased at her rebuff.

When Maddie came to the table, she gave me a quick smile. I smiled back. Jesse returned to his seat, shoved his glasses onto his face, and picked up Andrew's story.

"I'll go first," he said. He didn't look happy.

Andrew nervously chewed his pen. "I know you're, like, the god of this genre," he said. "But I hope the story's at least in your ballpark?"

I had a hard time biting my tongue at Andrew's anxious words. I was no Hemingway, and, yes, Jesse's writing was good—but not as good as he or Andrew thought it was. Still, though we were all honest and encouraging to Andrew, he only really listened to Jesse's feedback.

"It's a little, uh…rough." Jesse's tone was dismissive, bored. I could see the red marks he'd made all over Andrew's pages. "It's got issues. I'll go over some here, and you can look at the rest later."

"Oh. Okay." Andrew visually deflated, his expression wounded.

As Jesse related what he thought was wrong with the story, page by page, I watched Andrew slump deeper and deeper in his chair. I was appalled by Jesse's coldness, his taking Andrew apart, messing with him, just because he could, because he knew Andrew looked up to him. This seemed like a new low.

"I mean, with work it might have potential," Jesse said, finishing. "It's just been done a million times." He shrugged. "I don't know. Maybe other people liked it."

"I did," Maddie said defiantly.

I jumped in. "I liked it too. And I applaud Andrew for trying something new. Take it from someone who's been writing the same tired fantasy for years," I added with a chuckle.

"Tourists running around the jungle chased by cannibals?" Jesse smirked. "That's tired. What's the angle? Where's the story? Andy can do better."

"Seemed like a pretty good adventure tale to me," Walter said quietly.

Jesse didn't seem to hear him, turning to Andrew. "You can dig deeper, find whatever's in the story that's not coming out." He pointed to his head. "Dig in here. Your subconscious. I mean, there's a reason why we always talk about our dreams in relation to our writing, right? What we put on paper comes from our subconscious. And guess what? That's also dream territory, folks."

"It was going to be aliens!" Andrew blurted. He was about to cry. "A ship of grays…landing in the jungle. But…I couldn't."

"Andy? You okay?" Maddie asked him.

Andrew nodded, but he sipped his Red Bull with shaking hands. "I have nightmares. All the time. But I don't like to talk about them like you all do."

There was a pause. "Go for it, buddy," Jesse said. "We're all friends here." His switch in tone from criticizing to encouraging made me dizzy and suspicious.

"Well, I…dream about aliens a lot. Watching me with their eyes. Coming for me. Some nights I can't sleep." Andrew heaved a great sigh. "The worst nightmare I ever had was a few weeks ago. The gray aliens invaded…shooting people, eating…people, just this mass thing. They were ha…harvesting people. They took over the world, altering human DNA, changing them. And I was all alone, the only free human on the planet. And they knew it."

Maddie put her hand on Andrew's shoulder and gave him the kindest smile I've ever seen. "You're not alone, Andy," she murmured.

Andrew's eyes welled up. "I'm just afraid…if they catch me, if the grays catch me and kill me in my sleep…I'll die in real life."

"Hey, Andy, hey, buddy." Jesse's voice was soothing. "Maddie's right. Don't sweat it." He gave Andrew back his red-marked pages and then turned to the rest of the group. "But man, do I have a great idea. Check it out. We should compete…" He did his usual pause for dramatic effect. "…to see who can have the worst nightmare."

The gleam in his eyes disturbed me, and I should have said something, should have stopped it right then. But the idea intrigued me.

I said, "You can't make yourself have nightmares. They just happen."

But Walter was nodding. "Sometimes when I eat Mexican and have too many jalapeños, my dreams are really out of this world. Or how about watching scary movies? That makes everyone have nightmares, doesn't it?"

"Drinking too much coffee does it for me," I said. I watched Maddie's gaze flicker between Jesse and me. She still had her hand on Andrew's shoulder and seemed bewildered that we'd forgotten him.

"So that's a yes?" Jesse asked me.

"I'm…not sure."

Walter gave a shrug. "What the heck. I'll give it a try. Maybe it'll rev up my writing."

Andrew swiped a wrist across his wet eyes. "I'd rather not do it—is that okay?" He drew in a shuddering breath to compose himself. "I don't think I could do it."

"No problem, partner," Jesse said, and he flashed Andrew a grin. He looked at Maddie. "Maddie? You in?"

"I'll pass." Her tone was controlled. "I'm having enough trouble sleeping as it is."

Jesse held her eyes longer than I thought was necessary. I felt a clutching sensation in my chest, like my heart was being balled up in a tightly closing fist.

"I'm in," I said.

A smile spread across Jesse's face. "Bring it on." He

chuckled.

The rules were simple: try to have the worst nightmare you could anytime during the week, and tell it to the group at the meeting. The group would then vote on what they thought was the scariest. We'd be on the honor system, since there was no way we could prove a nightmare was genuine. The only participants were Jesse, Walter, and me, but everyone could vote if they wanted.

I decided to start by not sleeping for a night, then drinking cups of coffee until my hands shook and my head buzzed. My dreams the second night were jerky, disjointed. I remembered snatches of me yelling at my students in class, driving a strange flying car through heavy air traffic, and, of course, running into my old pal the giant, ravenous rat.

I didn't feel these would be enough to win. So the next evening, I ate spicy food, drank a six-pack of beer, and watched *The Shining*. Bored and wishing the movie were even half as good as the book, I fell asleep halfway through and didn't remember dreaming at all when I woke up.

The rest of the week, I came home from work too tired and stayed up too late correcting papers to even try. By the night of our group meeting, I hadn't had a real nightmare. I knew I needed to get better control of my dreaming.

Jesse came in that night looking haggard, and he drank two double-tall lattes during the course of the meeting. I told my dream about the flying car, which sounded watered down in the retelling. Walter's nightmare about singing the

National Anthem in front of fifty-thousand screaming hockey fans, though, had everybody in stitches.

"It was scary!" He wasn't happy at our reactions, but he finally cracked a smile.

Then Jesse told his nightmare. He'd dreamed he was climbing Mt. Rainier and a snowstorm appeared out of nowhere, leaving him stranded.

"The snow was blinding, swirling everywhere," he said, his hands making fluttering motions. "And then I heard a rumbling noise. I looked up…and it was just this wall of snow coming at me. An avalanche. It buried me. I just remember fighting the snow. Fighting and struggling…and being so cold. I couldn't breathe. And then…this giant claw came out of the snow…and grabbed my leg." He shot Andrew a look. "And then I woke up, thank God."

I noted the sarcasm in his last statement, but Andrew seemed oblivious, just sketching on his pad. He wasn't interested in the dream discussion, and only came alive after we'd voted (Jesse, of course, won) and moved on to talking about the week's manuscript pages.

Two nights later, as I sat at my computer working on my newest novel, a message popped in from Maddie: 'just saying hi.' I got up the nerve, dialed her number, and felt a little thrill go through my body when she answered.

"Are you doing the dumb competition, or are you writing?" she wanted to know.

"Both," I answered, glad to be able to say I was doing

at least a little writing. Maddie's continued encouragement since I joined the group had given me impetus to get more writing done, and I felt I'd actually finish the newest manuscript in record time.

"I thought I might…" she began, then faltered.

"Yes?"

"I thought I might give it a try. The competition. Just once." She laughed a little. "I mean, you all seem to think it's the best idea since sliced salami."

"You shouldn't," I said, and then it was my turn to stop abruptly.

"Really? Why not?" She sounded surprised.

"Because." I didn't have a concrete reason, just that it worried me, that she'd hurt herself somehow, that she'd hurt her writing. Or maybe it was that she'd be participating in something Jesse had suggested.

For a moment all I heard was her soft breathing on the other end of the line. Then there was the sound of liquid being poured into a glass.

"Well, I'm drinking wine," Maddie declared. "And if I drink enough of it, I have really weird dreams. I'm going to give it a shot tonight, the nightmare thing. If it doesn't work, no biggie."

The thought of her curled up in a chair, wine glass in her hand, her hair disheveled and her eyes bright, gave me such a feeling of longing I couldn't speak. I stood and went to the window, looking out at the clouds covering the stars.

"You're quiet," she said.

"I'm thinking." And then I took a deep breath. "I'm thinking we should go to a movie or something sometime."

She paused. "Sometime would be very cool," she replied.

We left it at that for now. She said things were a little manic at the moment, that she wasn't happy in her current relationship but hadn't actually discussed breaking up yet. I told her I understood.

During the next several writer's group meetings, we'd start by telling our worst nightmares of the previous week. Maddie participated just once, relating her recurring chair dream, but with a twist: she was outside the room looking in at the chair, and another woman, a stranger, was sitting in it. When the woman turned, she had no lower half of her face—as if it had been blown off with a shotgun or something. This upset Maddie enough to make her withdraw permanently from the competition.

Jesse won every time. Walter dropped out after a few weeks, but I kept trying. Most nights I dreaded going to sleep, at the same time wanting to win. But I couldn't quite reach Jesse's level of intensity. Each week Jesse and I looked more haggard and sleepy, and we both stopped writing.

This didn't sit well with the rest of the group. Though they seemed okay with the competition at first, soon they became less than understanding. Finally, tired of our bleary faces and lack of pages, they stopped voting and waited impatiently as we told our dreams, then moved on to writing-related discussions.

"This is, after all, a writer's group," Walter said one night a few months into the competition. "Shouldn't we get back to competing to see who can write the best stories?"

His usual wry humor had an edge to it, and I blearily nodded at him over my coffee. We were the first ones to arrive and so had the table to ourselves.

"You're right," I told him. "And in fact I've been doing research for a new novel."

"That's wonderful," Walter said. "Fantasy?"

I shook my head. "Thriller. A woman serial killer who pushes her victims out of windows but makes it look like suicide. So I've been learning about heights, and angles, and impact, fun things like that."

Walter chuckled. "Reading that would give me nightmares."

Everyone but Jesse arrived, and we were critiquing Andrew's newest chapters when Jesse came in an hour late and sat sullenly at the table. I'd been all set to tell what I decided would be my final nightmare in the competition, and I thought it would win, but we didn't discuss dreams that night.

"...So if you move up the chase in the tunnel to after Zahara reveals she's pregnant," Walter was saying, "there's more tension, because now we know Brandon is the father—"

"Brandon?" Jesse asked. "I don't remember a Brandon."

"The guy Zahara was dating before he became an alien," Walter patiently replied.

Jesse let out a cackle. "In your story there's an alien named Brandon? And he's bonking a chick named Zahara?" He nudged Andrew with his elbow. "That's hilarious."

Now both Walter and Maddie glared at Jesse. Andrew sank in his chair.

"Do you think aliens do it to John Williams soundtracks?" Jesse asked. He was on a roll.

I almost stood up. "Come on. Let Walter finish."

The codger continued. "So when Brandon catches Zahara and she tells him it's his baby, he of course doesn't care, which is good—"

Jesse laughed again. "Seriously, dude, what are you writing? The Real Housewives of ET? BEM 90210? Didn't we discuss the thing about reaching into your soul and finding—"

"Jesse, shut up." We all turned at Maddie's flat but deadly tone. The look she gave Jesse seemed more hurt than angry. "If you could write half as well as Andy, you wouldn't know what to do with yourself."

"The great writer lowers herself to speak to me," Jesse said. He cocked his head. "What an honor."

"Cram it, jerk," Maddie replied.

Andrew seemed like he was going to cry again. "Not

everyone has a killer instinct about everything, Jesse. I just…I just want to write, ya know? I'm not sure I even want to be published. I just love to write."

Jesse snorted. "Cripes. Man up, you big girl."

Walter rapped his hand three times on the table, like a judge with a gavel. "Okay, people. Maybe it's the moon. Maybe it's the air. But whatever it is, we're all a little cranky, obviously. Let's just call it a night and try again next week."

"Good idea," I said.

But Andrew stopped by my place a few days later and told me he was quitting the group. I tried to joke him out of it, promising to let everyone beat up Jesse while Andrew watched.

He gave a faint smile. "It's not about…the other night," he said in his hesitant voice. "It's more like…I don't know, Ned. This nightmare thing. It's not good."

"We don't have to talk about the dreams during meetings," I replied. I'd realized something in the last few days that I didn't like about myself, but there it was: I didn't want the competition to end. Not until I'd won, anyway.

Andrew just earnestly shook my hand. "Keep writing, okay?"

"You too, Andy," I replied, somber.

When I sat down to the next meeting, Walter was already there. Maddie and Jesse walked in the door at the same time, and my heart lurched as I thought they'd come together. Then I saw both of their cars in the parking lot and noticed they weren't speaking, and I breathed a little easier.

"Man, did I have the nightmare of all nightmares," Jesse said. His eyes were tinged red, his face slack, and I wondered if he was drunk.

As I told everyone about Andrew's quitting, Jesse only shrugged, morose, and stared into his coffee.

But Maddie quietly stood, and for the first time I noticed how tired she looked. "I think...I'm going to try writing on my own for a while," she said. "I love you all, I really do, but this group thing isn't helping me anymore."

Walter sadly shook his head. "Not you too."

I felt my insides split into a million pieces. "Maddie, no."

"I'm sorry—"

"You're the only thing keeping me writing at this point." I tried to take her hand, not caring if anyone at the table saw. "Please stay."

There was a clatter as Jesse clumsily rose to his feet and knocked over his coffee cup. Black liquid dribbled out. A couple at a nearby table looked up curiously.

"Go on then, Mad. What's taking you so long?" His words were slurred, and now I knew he'd been drinking. "You always desert everybody, don't you?"

Tears sprang to her eyes, and she grabbed her bag. "Only when they're beyond hope," she retorted.

"But—" and then my mouth was frozen. It couldn't be,

but there it was. Jesse and Maddie had been having…something, some kind of relationship, right under my nose, the signs so obvious and yet I had been blind to them. I was furious. I was sick.

"Bye, everybody," she muttered, and headed for the door.

"You know what, Maddie?" Jesse said, shouting. "Remember when you told Andrew he wasn't alone? Well, that's bullshit, and you know it. We are alone, all of us. All of us, Maddie!"

Walter and I sat in stunned silence as Jesse fell back into his chair and glared at his overturned coffee cup. And then we got our stuff together and just walked out. In the parking lot, Walter said he wanted to spend more time with his grandkids, and I said I understood.

And that was that. The group was over. And after a while, we lost touch.

I tried to keep writing, but mostly I just researched a few ideas. And I continued to write down my dreams, though I no longer tried to have nightmares.

But I couldn't get Maddie out of my head, and so I called her one night and we got together for a drink. When I asked her about Jesse, she confessed they'd seen each other awhile outside of the group, but she'd realized it wasn't going to work out.

"He mostly wanted to talk about nightmares, anyway," she told me. "He wants to control them, through hypnotism or combinations of drugs, whatever it takes. He hung out with some dangerous people." Maddie shuddered. "That's obsessed."

"Did it work?"

The look she gave me was like tiny daggers through my eyes.

"Never mind," I said with an embarrassed laugh. She didn't need to know I still fell asleep every night wondering what I'd dream about and hoping it would top anything Jesse had described during the competition.

The next night I asked Maddie on a real date, and she accepted. And then another, and she accepted again. As our relationship developed, I stopped writing down my worst dreams. In fact, as the months went by, I almost forgot about the nightmare competition altogether. We never mentioned Jesse, and I almost forgot about him as well.

Until one night I was checking my email and noticed one with the subject line 'Hi Ned its Jesse.' It had been a year since the writer's group broke up. Maddie had moved in with me a few months before, and things were going pretty well. She'd had a novel accepted for publication and was busy writing the sequel. I'd been promoted to guidance counselor at the high school and was slogging through my own novel. We'd talked about marriage.

My finger poised above the delete key, I thought about Jesse on that last night the group had gotten together. He'd had the nightmare of all nightmares, he'd said. And I'd been dying to tell my latest one too. I'd wanted to win once, just once. Now, of course, none of it mattered. But I was still curious.

My finger hovered, then pushed a key, and I opened his email.

He said he was in town and wanted to go out for a beer, if I was speaking to him. He apologized for the craziness he pushed on everyone. And he said he wanted to collaborate on a writing project. I was intrigued, and I wrote back. I didn't mention Maddie.

And I didn't tell Maddie about Jesse when I went out that night, just that I needed to pick up a few papers I'd forgotten in my office and not to wait up.

Jesse had given directions to a rundown bar on the waterfront, and it was already dark when I parked and nervously went in. This neighborhood, with its rusted warehouses, broken sidewalks, and dilapidated buildings, had escaped the inevitable renaissance of most city waterfront districts and seemed downright dangerous.

Looking even more pale and haggard than the last time I'd seen him, Jesse ordered a beer for me and a whiskey for himself. His eyes had an unhealthy brightness, and I noticed even in the dimly lit bar that his pupils were pinpoints.

"So this is what I'm thinking," he said, wasting no time launching into his idea. "I want to write a book about the nightmare competition. I've been researching all sorts of cool shit, stuff you wouldn't believe, and this book would be a runaway bestseller. Better yet, it would completely freak out everybody." He downed his shot of whiskey. "What do you think, bud?"

I didn't want to admit I was interested. "You've been trying to have nightmares again? Because we never really resolved the compet—"

"Again? Ah, hell, I never stopped." He grinned. "But I'll let you in on a little secret. Back then? I made up most of them, just to win."

"But…" Maybe I'd suspected all along, but it was still startling to hear Jesse admit it. I was pissed. I was hurt. "I…I never did," I said. "I never cheated."

"Why does it matter?" Jesse motioned to the bartender for another drink, then leaned toward me, his breath smelling of whiskey. "That bullshit's in the past. What I'm working on now blows all that out of the water."

"What are you working on?" I couldn't help myself. I'd wanted to win fair and square. I hated him so much. But I needed to know.

His eyes got narrow and sly. "Control, Ned," he said. "Creating nightmares in other people, and then controlling them."

I let out a laugh. "That's impossible. You'd have to hook up people to machines or something. Or hypnotize them."

"Oh, it's possible. Sort of astral projecting, and then injecting. You can be in their head all night, doing whatever you want, manipulating what happens. You can royally mess with them. And you leave when they wake up. You can't leave until they wake up, that's the hitch I'm still working out. You can help me with that."

He was serious. He was actually dead serious. I took a drink, noticing my reflection in the bar's mirror. And suddenly I was tired of playing. I had a life now. I had Maddie. How could I think of ruining that? What the hell was I wasting my time with Jesse for?

"Look," I said, "I know a few people who'd be happy to talk to you and help you. I can write down their numbers."

Jesse clumsily slammed his glass on the bar. "I don't need your pity. This is a legitimate business enterprise—"

"You just told me you lied about the nightmares. Now you expect me to believe you about this?"

Jesse regarded me. "It's all about control, isn't it, Ned? All about who's got the power." He grinned. "How's that giant rat treatin' ya?"

It sounded like a threat. I'd had enough, and I slid off my stool and tossed some bills on the bar. "You're the most self-involved person I've ever met. I'm done, okay?"

Jesse seemed genuinely hurt. I honestly didn't think he could feel that emotion. But he shrugged it off fast. "No sweat, pal," he said. "I've already got a publisher interested. Just thought you might want in on it. I know you've always wanted to be published."

As I left the bar, I heard him chuckling behind me.

Maddie was already in bed when I got home. I took some aspirin and climbed in next to her, rubbing my aching head. I was out like a light.

Jesse was suddenly in the room. I could hear him stumbling around in the dark, swearing, knocking over furniture. I opened bleary eyes and was surprised to see it was morning. Maddie was sitting up in bed. I smiled at her, but she was looking past me at something—

Jesse came up behind me, pushed me aside and grabbed Maddie by the hair, yanking back her head and slicing hard with a knife across her throat—

Blood spurted as I screamed—

And I opened my eyes. I smelled coffee and bacon, and I heard Maddie humming to herself downstairs.

"Morning, sweetie," she said as I cautiously came into the kitchen. I must have looked freaked, because she asked what was wrong. I started to describe my nightmare, but when I mentioned Jesse, her mouth went tight and she turned away. I decided not to tell her the rest, or about meeting him the night before.

Every night for three weeks, Jesse invaded my dreams and turned them into nightmares. I dreamed I was driving, and he was suddenly in the back seat covering my eyes with his hands. I dreamed about teaching, and he showed up in class and heckled me, then threw books at me. The worst dreams involved Maddie, and the things he did to her were so horrible I often woke up shouting and crying.

I messaged Jesse a dozen times, but he didn't reply. I went by the waterfront bar a few evenings, but he wasn't there. I even wandered the nearby streets, often at night, the very real fear nothing compared to the helpless fear of my nightmares and what Jesse might do in them.

Most nights I stayed awake as long as I could or didn't sleep at all. Maddie tried to talk to me, but I couldn't discuss Jesse knowing how it would upset her. I tried to nap at work in between classes, but Jesse found me there too. One day in my dream he walked into class carrying Maddie's severed head.

The next night he finally replied to my message, and we met again on the waterfront. I'd had three shots of whiskey by the time he decided to show up.

"I believe you," I said.

Jesse's sly grin was back. "You want to know how?"

I knocked back one more shot of liquor and nodded, fighting the urge to break the glass and shove it, jagged, into Jesse's unbelievably gaunt face.

I went with him to a place just down the alley where a sign on the weathered door read 'Fortunes.' Inside, the incense was so thick I could barely breathe. A frowning woman in jeans and a sweatshirt with cats on it sat at a folding table, cards splayed out in front of her. I noticed they were a hand of solitaire. When she saw Jesse, she frowned even more and pointed to a doorway behind her.

"Fortune?" she asked me with little enthusiasm.

"No, thanks," I said. My words slurred.

As I followed Jesse to the back room, she touched my arm. "You'll be able to sleep soon," she said.

Lucky guess, I thought. She saw I looked tired.

Her husband's face had the deepest crags I'd ever seen. His small black eyes constantly shifted around the room but didn't meet mine or Jesse's. He said dreams were codes that could be unlocked if you got under their skin, that nightmares were dark worlds with heads for doors. He said Jesse was a savant, but he could teach me the tricks too—for the right price.

"Tricks?" I repeated. I didn't feel well. My head swam from incense smoke and four shots of whiskey.

Jesse's face spun and whirled in front of me. "You should have said yes, Ned. A crying shame. This book will make me rich. I wonder who'll play me in the movie."

"You're not going to stop, are you?" A question, but I knew the answer.

"No," Jesse replied. "Not with you, and not with Maddie."

"You're a sick bastard," I whispered. And passed out.

I awoke to smoke, but this time it wasn't incense. A firefighter was dragging me out of the burning building. The man and his wife were in ambulances. Jesse was nowhere to be seen—

And wanted for arson.

After the hospital checked me out, I went home and

woke up Maddie. I asked her about Jesse, and she broke down in tears, confessing he'd messaged her too and they'd met once for coffee.

"Nothing happened, Ned," she said. "I swear. He was a total mess, and all he talked about was you. You and the nightmares and the stupid competition." She was crying hard now. "Why can't you just give this up? Please, Ned. Why are you so obsessed with this…this utter shit?"

I had to know one other thing. "Have you been dreaming about him? Has he been in your dreams?"

"My dreams? No. God, isn't it bad enough that he's taken over our waking lives?"

I sat down suddenly, weak with relief. "Yes. Yes, it is."

My relief was short-lived. Maddie and I started to drift apart, not talking much, not sleeping together. I barely slept anyway, and I know she thought I was trying to have nightmares again. The looks she gave me broke my heart.

Several nights later, when I jolted awake from Jesse's latest nightmare and wouldn't tell Maddie why I'd been screaming in my sleep, she packed up a few things and said it was better if she stayed with her mother for a week or so. But a week became two, and then three. Our phone calls became shorter and more polite, less familiar.

The house was empty with her gone. Most nights I tried to write or do research, but often I ended up sitting at the bedroom window looking out at the clouds covering the stars.

Late one night, I nursed a tall glass of whiskey and sat on the windowsill, my legs dangling above two stories to the sidewalk below. I thought about all that had happened, how I'd wanted to sell a novel or two, how I'd wanted to get down on one knee and propose to Maddie the right way, build a life together. Now it was all gone, all of it.

You can be obsessed with love. You can be obsessed with a lust for power, for control. And you can be obsessed with competing and winning at all costs. In my case, my obsession was represented in my dreams by a giant pet rat named Elliott who waited for me in the garage of my childhood.

I looked down at the sidewalk. All that research I'd done for my latest novel, and now it would never be written. But maybe that was okay. I set my glass carefully on the floor, leaned backward out the open window…and let myself fall.

—

In my dream, I was floating above a field of daisies. Maddie told me once they were her favorite flower. In the distance I could see a house. As I got nearer, I realized it was the house I grew up in.

The garage door was open, and when I touched down the daisies were suddenly gone, replaced by concrete. I walked to the open garage door, feeling occasional tiny stones under my bare feet, but they didn't hurt.

I heard a noise from inside the garage, a low, throaty

growl, and I knew I should be scared. But I wasn't. Not anymore. Then Jesse appeared in the doorway, grinning in his usual triumphant way, saying "Hi, Ned," and coming out to meet me.

There he was, I thought. And behind him were a dozen giant rats, as big as St. Bernards, and they all had dripping fangs and blazing eyes. A dozen Elliotts, all ready to rip me to pieces for letting them suffer in a cramped, dirty cage. Jesse's rodent army.

One of the rats lunged for me, but I beat it back with the club that suddenly appeared in my hand. Then another one lunged, and I beat that one back.

The rest of the giant rats noticed something behind me. They began to chatter, confused and scared. Some edged away.

Jesse looked surprised, and as I came steadily toward him, I explained a few things. How I'd been doing my own research on controlling dreams. Lucid dreaming, they called it. A fascinating subject.

And how we'd have plenty of time to see if I'd mastered the technique, because we'd both be spending a long time in dreamland.

"What…what do you mean?" Jesse asked, shifting on his feet, nervous. Now he looked past me, behind me, and he saw what the rats saw.

"I've been doing other research too, buddy," I told him. "About heights, and about angles, and about what impact is needed to induce coma but not death. I fell out the window just right, hit my head just right so that my brain function wasn't too impaired." I walked toward him, hoisting the club. "I'm in a mild coma, Jesse, old pal. And it should last a good long while."

Jesse screamed. I could hear it as if he were actually right in front of me and not just trapped in my nightmare. Trapped, and with a thousand gray aliens, giant bug eyes smiling, long fingers reaching, swarming past me right toward him. They shot yellow beams out of their eyes, grabbing the rats as they scattered, busily wrapping the giant shrieking rodents in wet pod casings for later consumption.

When Jesse ran, I just smiled. How far could he go? Besides, I had all the time in the world to find him. What else was there but time, when the only thing you could do was sleep and dream and not wake up?

THE EDITOR

You get coffee. You glance around. A dozen people sip beverages and stare into their computers.

You sit. Then you spot him.

He's at the counter. He looks at the menu board. You watch him order, watch him pay.

"Thank you," he says with a smile. "Have a great day."

You press buttons on your device.

He's terse the second time. "Thanks." No smile.

You watch him take his coffee and sit. He drinks his coffee, scrolls messages on his phone. His movements are fluid, natural. Whoever built him did a good job.

After a moment he raises his head and looks at the people in the coffeeshop. His expression is open, friendly. He smiles at a mother and child sharing cocoa.

You press buttons on your device. His expression turns blank. He goes back to his phone.

Eventually he stands, walks to the recycle bin. His hand hovers. You press buttons on your device. He moves to the other bin and drops his cup into the overflowing trash.

Outside, cars move like sludge, trapped by traffic lights. The sidewalk throngs with busy people, eyes straight ahead or on their phones.

You watch him fall into step with the other pedestrians,

walk briskly. You follow a few feet behind. His gait is seamless, no noticeable errors there. You send a note to your supervisors telling them you're impressed with his construction.

He walks by storefronts and gray towering buildings. Then he slows and swivels his head. There's a bird in a tree, singing. He's listening with a rapt expression. You sigh and press buttons on your device. He strides past the tree and doesn't pay attention to the bird.

Ahead, the sudden blare of a car horn, the squeal of brakes. A shriek of pain cut short.

He hurries toward the growing crowd of onlookers. In the street, cars have stopped. Behind the wheel of a sedan a woman sits dazed.

Partway under the woman's car splays a little girl, bleeding, moaning. The onlookers pull out their phones, snap pictures, gawk, snap more pictures.

You watch him push through the crowd. He pulls out his phone. But he doesn't take pictures.

You watch him rush to the street.

You watch him kneel beside the moaning little girl and punch 9-1-1 into his phone, talk urgently. He leans down to check the little girl.

You inform your supervisors this one will need a complete rewrite. He isn't acting like a human. Then you delete him.

BITTY

Bitty likes the barn cats. She follows them around the yard whenever I let her out of her pen. I'm not supposed to let her out. The first few times Dad gave Bitty a whipping. Now I let Bitty out in secret but I put her back in soon as I hear Dad coming down the path. Bitty smiles every time and gives me a pat on the arm, and I feel like a good big sister.

When I let Bitty out, she wants to go down to the pond a ways behind the barn. At first I was scared she'd fall in and drown. There's weeds that can tangle and catch you. But Bitty knows enough not to go to the edge. She's really strong anyway. She could probably pull herself right out of those weeds if she had to.

Sometimes I sit with her by the pond and brush her hair. I make Mama cut mine short, but Bitty's hair is long and wild 'cause nobody tends it. Bitty tries to brush it, but with so many arms like she's got it's hard I guess. Sometimes we listen to the birds and other times we sing songs. Bitty can't really sing but she makes hums. Then she looks in my eyes and does her noises and I know she's trying to talk but she can't.

Before Bitty goes to sit by the pond, she looks for the cats. If they're not in the yard, she sneaks in the barn. She meows and gets on the wood floor and plays. Those barn cats are sometimes so wild you can't pet them, but Bitty is quick and almost always gets hold of one. She pets it and makes her coo noises. She likes the kittens best. She closes her eyes and smiles and I know she's so happy right then. It makes me feel good. Bitty isn't happy much being in her pen and the little shed Dad built. There's chains in the shed, and Dad goes in there and makes sure Bitty stays chained all night.

One time Bitty took a kitten to sit with her by the pond. By the time I got there the kitten wasn't moving and there was blood. At first she didn't know what she had done. I told her no Bitty that was too rough play gentle, play gentle. I guess she listens 'cause I'm her big sister. She got it right away and there hasn't been another time.

I buried the kitten in a pretty field near the woods. There's brown grass up to my waist, and pieces of a fencepost I made into a cross. I got Dad's shovel and dug a grave. My arms got tired, but I had to do it so Dad didn't find out and give Bitty a whipping. I forgot to put something over the kitty's face and dirt got in its eyes. I felt bad. I think Bitty felt bad too.

Dad and Mama and me and Wade, my little brother, live in the house. Wade turned three in April. Mom calls Wade a pistol. She's always chasing him. But she doesn't let him near the shed that's for sure. One time Wade did wander too near the shed and Mama screamed 'cause all of

Bitty's arms reached out the window and quick almost caught him. Dad scooped him up just in time, but I don't think Bitty would hurt him. Mama's got a big, round tummy, and that means she's gonna have a baby, just like one of the barn cats, my favorite one I named Dandelion.

    Dandelion is so light orange she's yellow, and she's got half an ear missing. But she's sweet and smart and she's gonna be a good mama. I asked Dad if I could keep one of Dandelion's kittens in the house and let it sleep in my bed, but he said no. That made me sad. I didn't want to cry in front of him so I went to the barn and cried. I told Dandelion if she has a white kitten I'll name it Snow and if she has a gray kitten I'll name it Mist.

    I remember a long time ago Bitty slept in my bed. That was when Bitty lived in the house with us. She was really little and wasn't like she is now. I would hold her to me just like a kitten and we would fall asleep listening to the crickets out the window. Then she grew un-atcheral, and Mama and Dad had long talks about what to do. Then Dad built Bitty's pen.

    When Bitty was Wade's age, Mama made her a cat costume. It was a tiger cat, and it had four mitten paws and a hood with fuzzy ears. Dad took us trick-or-treating in the car all around for miles. I was a witch but I was a good witch. That was a good night, Mama even said so. She said there, now Bitty's covered up and nobody will even know. We went to all the neighbors and they gave us candy and said Bitty was such a sweet kitty-cat. Bitty meowed and they laughed, and Bitty smiled and they said my what sharp kitty teeth you have! Dad didn't look happy at that last part and quick got back in the car and said Bitty you be quiet and don't open your mouth. But it was still a good night.

Dad says Bitty is dee-monic. He doesn't say it when Mama is around, though. I don't know what it means, but I know it's bad. I think it's like dee-formed. That's another word Dad calls Bitty, and Mama does too. Sometimes Dad says they should just let the thorities come and take Bitty away, but Mama doesn't like it when he says that.

This Halloween, Bitty grew too big and didn't fit in her cat costume, so Wade was the kitty this year. Mama sewed up a rip in the sleeve and it was good as new. We took pictures. I was a princess. Dad put on a monster mask, and Mama wore all orange and her tummy looked like a pumpkin. Dad took me and Wade trick-or-treating but not Bitty. It wasn't as much fun, but Dad said Bitty didn't have a costume so she couldn't go.

I could hear Bitty making her sad noises from her pen when we walked to the car.

This morning I saw Bitty's face at her shed window. She was howling to beat the devil so I let her out. She can't reach the latch to the pen but she's strong enough to pull her chains out of the wall. I don't say anything, though, 'cause if Dad knew she'd get a whipping.

We played by the pond and I told her about how

Dandelion was gonna be a mama soon and have kittens. Bitty got so excited all her arms started going all around in the air and she made her happy coo noises.

On the way back up the path, Dad saw Bitty out of her pen and he got mad. What the hell he said did she get out by herself. I said I let her out I'm sorry.

Dandelion ran in his way. I couldn't get her quick enough and Dad kicked her right in her tummy. I screamed. Dad only got madder and said you both get a whipping so you both get in the shed. He did the chains on Bitty and then got the whip and said to me you just stay there. Then he went for Bitty with the whip.

Bitty didn't even cry. She looked at me. The whip cut in her skin deep and green spilled out. Dad made a disgusted noise.

I said it quick I said play rough Bitty play rough. She knew what I meant and she pulled the chains out of the wall. She's strong. I didn't watch after that though. I went outside and listened to the screams for a while and then they stopped.

I walked down to the barn and Dandelion was crying and having her kittens, four of them. I helped her. One was born dead 'cause of the kicking, but the others looked okay. One is gray. I'm so happy. When they get older, I'm gonna let Bitty pick one for her very own. I know she'll be gentle with it.

I don't know if I should bury Dad in the pretty field

near the woods or put him in the pond. Mama won't be able to find Dad if he's in the field. But if he's in the pond, maybe she'll think he got tangled in the weeds and drowned.

Then the thorities won't come and take Bitty away.

DIGESTIBLE

Monday, March 7:

Hi, loyal readers! Remember last week how I blogged about that guy in front of me at the salad bar who held the tongs hostage so long they developed Stockholm syndrome? Well, today he took for...ev...rrr to arrange his cherry tomatoes on their bed of lettuce so they would artistically complement the shredded cheese and croutons.

Slow people in the salad line, please: you're not painting the Sistine flippin' Chapel! You're throwing vegetables on a plate to shove in your craw—then they're all jumbled together in your gut anyway before bobsledding through a mile of intestines toward the inevitable finish line. So move it—there are people behind you!

Now to the coolest news in the galaxy, literally! Triffitz Corp., everyone's favorite interplanetary wholesaler, has finally introduced their new meat into stores and restaurants. And our downstairs cafeteria too! We're not talking the lab-grown stuff, synthetic meat, shmeat. No, sir—this is real animal, direct from Titan or Io. Or Callisto. One of those moons of Saturn. Or Jupiter.

So I skipped the salad bar and had an alien burger, and it was uh-may-zing! Tender. Juicy. Waited in line there, too, but it was worth it! Triffitz Corp. promises the end of boring meals, and boy do they deliver. It's just like any other meat, so you can cook it however you like. And the best part is they claim it tastes different to everyone who eats it!

I thought my burger tasted like bacon meets chocolate meets the best steak I've ever had. My coworker Brian said his tasted like his mom's home-fried chicken. A woman in the elevator compared hers to pepperoni pizza. Gonna have to pick some up for dinner!

Thursday, March 10:

Miss me, bloggees? I was in bed with the biggest, ugliest stomach bug! Even missed work. But today I'm back, and my appetite's back too. You know what lunch is gonna be, don'tcha? You got it!

Did you see the press release from Triffitz Corp.? There's already a shortage of alien meat due to popular demand—even with the European boycott (they think it's GMO or some nonsense). But hang on! Triffitz reassures us that a ship full of live alien food animals is zipping its way to Earth right now. They've got farms set up across the country, cuz according to Triffitz these things breed like bunnies, despite being as big and plump as cows and not cute at all. So we'll never have a shortage again!

Tuesday, March 15:

Lots of people out sick today. Rumors are flying that Triffitz burgers are just not agreeing with everybody. Sort of like a meaty Montezuma's revenge. (And, yes, I know how un-PC that was.) I've had a few bouts of heartburn myself, but antacids clear it right up! Am headed out to lunch—guess what I'm having!

Saturday, March 19:

Um, yeah, Triffitz Corp. should have studied the alien species longer. Maybe done a little more testing. I mean, just because you kill something and chop it up and cook it at 160 degrees doesn't mean it's dead. I've had like fifteen burgers in the past couple of weeks, so by now my insides are goo on their way to slurry. If you've eaten any alien meat, even only a bite of it, doesn't matter—it's already taking its comestible joyride through your organs. And it won't stop.

Yep. Turns out while we've been eating them...they've been eating us.

BLUNDER

The sun was sinking behind the San Jacinto mountains as Rankin drove his Audi along Milky Way and turned right onto Mars Avenue on his way to Comet Lane. He had a tenant who owed him back rent, and he was coming to collect.

The mobile home park was Rankin's brainchild. When he'd bought the property some years before—ten short streets and three cul-de-sacs of vintage trailers, built in the 1960s—things were rusty and run down. The night Rankin signed the park mortgage, and as it happened also his divorce papers, the jimmy leg was the worst it had ever been. He'd stared out the window for hours, jittering his legs and pounding on his thighs to kill the creeping, the itching. And as he'd gazed at the moon, it hit him.

The next day Rankin named the streets after heavenly bodies, added atomic age signage, and called the place Galaxy Motor Park. It gave the property a hook. Rankin also booted freeloading tenants or undesirables who didn't keep their yards clean. He even had to remove one mobile home as a toxic waste dump because of the meth lab. Now that lot was an off-leash dog minipark, very popular with the residents. And he was making money every month.

As Rankin turned left onto Comet Lane, he noticed a

bulb out in the streetlight. He'd get that fixed in the morning. This was one of the oldest streets in the park, so the trailers had a bit more vintage charm, the yards more overgrown with shrubs and cactus and palms. His overdrawn tenant Poppy Devane's trailer sat snug and homey at the end of the lane.

Rankin didn't mind a little funk in his park, a little kitsch. It was expected in a town like Palm Springs that boasted of its midcentury modern heritage. The mobile homes had character, and several residents had been living on Comet Lane since day one, some on low income and now on social security. Poppy herself had taken over her mother's trailer after the old lady died.

He even liked Poppy's latest décor. She'd painted the trailer a dark blue with aqua and lime trim, white painted stars amid the blue, and she'd hung white stars-and-moons Christmas lights that framed the roof of the porch and carport.

Poppy sometimes told fortunes, and Rankin didn't mind that either. But a few months before, she'd posted a sign that said 'Tattoos,' and Rankin was pretty sure she didn't have a business license for that. Even if she did, most of the clientele he'd happened to see going in and out at all hours were definitely undesirables.

Poppy's boyfriend, the gray-hair with a ponytail and Harley motorcycle, had left weeks earlier. So it was just her—and her son, who must be a teenager by now, but

Rankin had seen him only once, sitting on the couch playing *Resident Evil* on Xbox. A sullen, pudgy kid with shaggy hair.

Hell, Rankin thought, pulling up in front of Poppy's trailer and parking, even old enough to have a teenage kid, the mom wasn't half-bad. Forty was the new thirty, right? Rankin thought about Poppy sometimes, again if the jimmy leg was bad and he needed distraction. She usually wore tank tops, and he'd picture her freckled shoulders and lithe arms, and that would be enough to get him started. And finished.

Rankin went up the steps, his huaraches crunching on faded fake grass, and knocked on the aluminum front door. A cobweb sagged from the upper corner of the porch screen. Rankin reached up and swiped at the web, then shook it off his hand. A brown spider plopped onto the porch and started to scramble off.

But Rankin hurried to smash it with his foot. Then he grimaced as he scraped the dead thing off his shoe onto the step.

Poppy Devane appeared at the screen door. "Yes?" She blinked as if the sun, now just a fading aura over the mountains, hurt her eyes. "Oh, Mr. Rankin."

Her ginger hair was mussed, stray mascara smeared under her eyes. She'd just woken up, obviously. It was almost 6 p.m. Her black tank top was only partially tucked in her faded jeans.

Rankin put on his grin, the one reserved for tenants he was about to give bad news to. "Remember I said to call me Tom."

Hiding a yawn behind her hand, Poppy opened the screen door. "Do you want to come in?" She said it like it was an afterthought.

"I'll only be a minute," Rankin replied as he moved past her into the mobile home. He made sure his arm just barely brushed Poppy's breast as he stepped by.

Poppy usually kept the place tidy; he'd never faulted her housekeeping. The furniture was old, some of it obviously from yard sales, but she kept it clean. No dishes in the sink, no crumbs on the counter.

But now he noticed a few more cobwebs in the corners of the ceiling.

And he saw a pack of cigarettes and a lighter on the Formica table in the kitchenette, next to an ashtray with butts and ashes. He didn't remember Poppy smoked. Maybe it was the son.

"How's... I'm sorry, is it Kenny?"

"Kyler. He's good. He's in his room, I think." Poppy went to the kitchen table, hip touching the edge.

Poppy's crystal ball, tarot cards, and other New Agey crap were also on the table. And some sketches of butterflies in colored pencil, and dragonflies and ladybugs. For tattoos, presumably. The sketches looked amateur.

"How's your new business turning out?" Rankin asked.

"Oh, pretty good. I just did this on a friend of mine." Poppy pointed to one of the butterflies. "It isn't super complicated, and it turned out good. She said it made her feel like she could fly."

"Where did she have you put it?" His mind flashed to some places.

"On her shoulder. Here." Poppy turned around and put her fingertips on the back of her shoulder. She had no tats herself, only tanned, bare skin. And the freckles.

Rankin swallowed, his throat suddenly dry. He fought the urge to cover her hand with his own.

Poppy's fingers dropped, reached toward the pack of Marlboros, hesitated, then pulled away. She wandered into the living room.

"I bet I know why you're here." Her voice was tense and tight. "And I'm gonna ask a favor."

"A favor."

"I'm asking for two weeks more, just two weeks, because I have a client who's gonna pay me, he owes me for a complete sleeve—"

"Will it cover the amount you owe? You owe thirteen hundred and thirty dollars, Poppy."

"It'll cover a lot of that for sure, and I have a few more appointments this week."

"We had a very similar conversation last month."

"And I paid, right? I paid some of the money." She sighed. "Everything's so expensive these days. And there's my son too. It's hard keeping a teenager fed." Her eyes brimmed with tears. She swiped at them with her hand, smearing more mascara.

"Poppy."

"Please, Mr. Rankin. Things have been tough. I had some money stolen."

"The guy with the Harley?"

He expected Poppy to tell him it wasn't any of his business. But she only looked defeated. "I'm trying to get back on my feet," she finally murmured.

He thought her voice sounded huskier when she was about to cry. He liked it.

"I'm a patient man," Rankin said. "But there's a waiting list for space in this park, did you know that? Conscientious tenants with excellent references."

"This place is all I have. It's all Kyler has. We love it here."

"I'm not a charity, Poppy—"

"Please." Poppy held her hands out, begging. "Please, Mr. Rankin."

Rankin cocked his head. When he was in college, before his hair started prematurely thinning, he'd cock his head this way and a lock of unruly bangs would slip down and almost cover his eyes. The girls told him it was sexy.

"I thought I told you to call me Tom," Rankin said.

And that's all he needed to say. He could see in Poppy's eyes she understood the situation, what was going to need to happen in the next moments. She owed him—but there were other payments besides money, other ways to bargain.

He kept his eyes locked on Poppy's, moving toward her. She shivered, but she didn't break his gaze as she backed away toward the kitchenette. Not in a nervous way, he thought, but calmly, accepting.

Would it be against the counter? Or on the table among her tattoo drawings? Closeups flashed through his mind: colored-pencil butterflies glimpsed through Poppy's tousled hair, the freckles on her shoulders, her silky lashes framing her closed eyes.

Poppy's hip again touched the kitchen table and she stopped. Rankin came forward. Now they were two feet apart, no more. He felt his heart knocking against his chest.

She reached back and pulled a cigarette out of the pack and put it to her lips, flicked the lighter. Her eyes left his briefly to watch the flame burn the end of her cigarette. Rankin watched it too.

She extinguished the flame and inhaled deeply, then let the smoke trickle out. She looked thoughtful. Dreamy, even. Was she anticipating what was about to happen, like he was?

Rankin started to smile. His hand reached toward her shoulder. She was taller than he was, so he tilted his face up, leaning in.

Poppy again brought up the cigarette. Rankin had to tilt awkwardly backward. If he'd leaned closer, he would have been burned. Poppy didn't lower the cigarette, but held it in front of her lips. Rankin clenched his jaw. Now he was getting pissed.

Poppy said, "Mr. Rankin, when I get the money, I'll send a check. In a couple weeks."

He blinked. So she had just been getting a cigarette. She hadn't understood the situation at all. Or if she had, she was playing him. Well, screw that. He was taking his payment.

He reached for her, roughly, and it gave him satisfaction to see alarm in her eyes—

There was a click. A door opening, and Rankin noticed the bulky shape, presumably Poppy's kid Kyler, in the dimness of the back hallway. There was a blotch of a tattoo on the teen's arm. Rankin hastily pulled away from Poppy.

The kid shuffled out the back door of the trailer, closing it behind him. But Rankin could see a shape through the window. He was lingering outside near the door. Keeping an eye on him?

Rankin sighed. Fine. It wouldn't be tonight, Poppy and him. But it would be soon, he knew it. She was too inept with money for it not to.

Poppy had slipped around the table, putting it between them. Rankin slammed his fist on it, got more satisfaction watching her jump, startled.

"You have a week, or you're evicted." He headed for the door, pointing to the cobwebs near the ceiling. "And clean this place up!"

Once Rankin was on the porch, he gasped for air like he'd been suffocating. The rising full moon was a big, round mouth on the horizon. He stalked to his car, glancing up the quiet street. On Comet Lane the lines of trailers—his trailers—seemed tranquil and sleepy.

A noise behind him. Rankin turned to see through the tall prickly pear cactus in Poppy's side yard a square of amber light. She'd opened the window in the kitchenette.

Rankin couldn't help himself. He drifted to the brick path that meandered next to her trailer. The kid might be in the backyard, smoking or texting someone. But if Rankin was really quiet, he'd be undisturbed here and could catch a look through the window.

After Rankin had talked to Poppy last month, he'd crouched behind the palms and cactus of this side yard and watched her for quite a while. Back here the overgrowth had swallowed him up in its dark and quiet.

Rankin crept along the brick path, finding the place he'd hid before. He slipped between two potted palms taller than he was, but he suddenly couldn't go on, caught on something. A cactus? Then he felt the whispers of soft strands on his face. He tried to back away, but silky fibers caught his arms and shoulders and legs. He'd walked into a spider web.

Eyes adjusting to the dark, Rankin could see the web was huge, encompassing the space between the two palms and over four feet high. Fear plucked at his nerves. What kind of spider made a web like this?

Rankin flailed his arms but only got more ensnared in sticky fibers. He saw, through the prickly pear, Poppy standing at her kitchen window. She was still smoking, looking up at the moon. Should he call out? But if he did, she'd know he was creeping around outside.

There was a rustling as someone moved along the path. The son, Kyler, coming from the backyard.

"Hey," Rankin said, relieved. "I'm caught."

From the dark: "Sure are."

Rankin had never heard Poppy's son speak. His voice was scratchy and muffled, like it was an effort to talk. The kid came close and loomed above Rankin, standing over six feet. He wore a dirty T-shirt and torn jeans.

The kid reached out his arms—

But there weren't just two arms, Rankin saw. There were, dear God, eight. Eight arms with dark barbed hairs, hooked on the ends, and they started moving fast, busy, weaving strands of sticky silk the kid was pulling from under his T-shirt, from openings in his belly.

The kid moved into the light of the moon and he was a hideous monster, with bulbous dark eyes and spider mouth parts, but human enough Rankin could tell it was Poppy's kid all right. The splotch of a tattoo Rankin saw earlier was, ludicrously, a clumsily drawn spider.

Rankin lost it, lost all rational thought. "Hey, kid, no, kid," he babbled, "Let me go, look, let me go. You need money, you want the car, whatever you want—"

The kid opened a huge, hairy mouth like a maw. Rankin screamed but it came out high and breathy. His scream stopped short as, in a blur, the kid moved in and bit Rankin's head, then bit him again.

Rankin felt searing pain—then it was like warm whiskey pumping down through his veins, and he felt weak.

He tried to thrash his arms, but they were quickly becoming constricted to his sides. Past the kid's weaving, hooked claws and strands of silk growing over his own face, Rankin saw Poppy shut the window and turn away and disappear inside her trailer.

"Please...please..." Rankin started, but that's all he could get out. His throat was tightening, and it was hard to breathe. His tongue swelled like a giant leech, filling his mouth. His vision swam.

Rankin rotated then, as the giant spider kid continued to wrap him up like a mummy. No, not a mummy—like a bug in a web. Poppy's side yard spun.

"You killed...my friend," the kid said.

For a moment Rankin couldn't figure out what that meant. Then he realized—the spider he'd squashed on the front porch. And he realized something else. The kid knew Rankin had been back here before, spying on his mother. And tonight he'd caught him.

Rankin stopped spinning. The freak spider kid leaned down close to Rankin's stomach, his head smelling like unwashed hair and rotted meat. His mouth parts bit again, and a wet pain sluiced through Rankin's gut. Rankin felt queasy in hot, fluid bursts.

His insides were liquefying.

The kid's mouth parts sucked loudly, eating Rankin's organs like slurry.

Rankin's legs collapsed under him. Good thing he was so bound he couldn't fall. He twisted his head in the web and raised his eyes to the full moon. That was all Rankin saw for the next remaining moments, until he saw nothing.

RABBIT

Tanner used to run. The medals he'd won in high school and college track then collected dust on his bedroom dresser for years. After he told his last girlfriend he was leaving her, she threw them all in the recycling. By that time Tanner was fifty pounds overweight and didn't want to look at them anymore anyway.

When Tanner's doctor said he had high blood pressure and quoted statistics about overweight older men with high blood pressure, Tanner started walking. There was a park ten minutes from his house, with a lake and a boat launch and ducks and geese. Farther along there were paved paths and trails lined with maples and firs and flowering trees.

So Tanner walked. He took his blood pressure twice a day with one of those wrist jobs. And in a few months Tanner's numbers went down and his doctor was happy. Tanner stopped taking the meds, too, though the doctor didn't know that part.

Not that it mattered much, because asteroids were hurtling toward Earth. Three of them, big as skyscrapers. That was the good news—that they weren't bigger. So there was a chance much of the United States would survive. Scientists estimated at least two would hit the West Coast, flattening cities and towns between California and

Vancouver, BC, and impacting inland two hundred miles or more. The third would land in the Pacific Ocean, they said, so expect an epic tsunami to wipe clean what might to be left of the Pacific Northwest.

The scientists took their findings to the President, who decided the Pentagon and the military knew more, reassuring everyone they'd find a solution. They'd shoot the asteroids down or blow them up or divert them. Money was the issue right now. So the scientists waited, their hands tied.

In the meantime, jokes about oceanfront property in Arizona aside, a steady migration of people, their electronics, and their pets had already started moving east.

Tanner decided to stay awhile, see if the solution arrived or the first wave of migrations waned. It was scary to wait, though, boy howdy. And Tanner had no one to share the fear with. Fourteen years since he left his wife. Eight since he walked out on his girlfriend. He'd heard the same thing from both of them—he was distant. He wasn't "there." After hearing that, he made damn sure "there" was the last place he'd be.

The walking helped douse the memories—some days Tanner really poured it on, gasping by the time he found a shady place to rest. His favorite spot was along a pile of boulders, a retaining wall shoring up a bank of trees, where he liked to park it and catch his breath.

The first few times the rabbit popped out from among

the boulders and noticed Tanner sitting on the wall, it turned easy as you please, not in a hurry, and slid back into the hole, not panicked, just wary. It had smaller, more delicate ears than Tanner thought rabbits had, and dark tips to its tawny gray fur.

Then as the days went by, it got so the rabbit would hop around a bit and eat and watch Tanner, cautious but enjoying the slivers of green grass between its gentle lips. Its brown eyes were wise. Its sweet demeanor brightened Tanner's day. Sometimes he even found himself smiling.

Ten years into his marriage, Tanner's wife had told him he never smiled at her or at anything she did. Tanner realized this was true, and it was because there was no joy there, no grace. The relationship had grown boring, just work and not much else. A year after Tanner left, he happened to see her at a table across a busy restaurant, smiling and laughing with her friends. He realized what a jerk he'd been and slunk off to another restaurant.

The government finally found the funds and gave the go-ahead, and rockets were deployed to deflect the asteroids' trajectories. It worked, they said. Less of the West Coast would be destroyed, they said. But the asteroids were now too close to try again. The rockets might deflect the asteroids straight toward Earth. If only they'd had more time, they said. And the President and the Pentagon then shrugged their collective shoulders and retreated to their secret bunkers.

The scientists announced the day and time of arrival, assuring 90 percent accuracy. Evacuations of the West Coast began in earnest. But Tanner found himself wondering what would happen to the little rabbit at the park. Maybe hiding in its hole between the boulders it would survive the impact, but then what? Would it be able to breathe, to find food?

Tanner read up on it. Some said there would be nuclear winter. Some said there would be cataclysmic earthquakes. Some said little green aliens would climb out of the smoldering rubble and start auditioning sex slaves. It was hard to find facts in the middle of all the panic and conjecture, but one thing was certain: people were running. Tanner would too.

He would pack the car with only the essentials. He would drive nonstop to Jackson Hole, Wyoming, and then straight east until the Atlantic Ocean. But every road and highway was clogged with vehicles 24/7, so Tanner decided to wait. He had almost three weeks.

He still took his daily walks. It helped with the rising panic. But he also walked because it felt good, and there wasn't much else in this world that did. Afterward he'd sit on the retaining wall and watch the rabbit. It started to think of Tanner as part of the scenery and went about hopping, sniffing, eating, playing. Just being a rabbit. Not many people came by anymore, and they both enjoyed the quiet.

Tanner's last girlfriend had been a talker. More

accurately, a mumbler, so Tanner was always asking "What?" That got on his nerves. Hers too, he guessed. Then there was the drama. Many times he'd come home to find her tossing his belongings in the trash or out the window. Once she mumbled something about how they didn't connect. He asked, "What?" and she threw a desk lamp at him. The lamp did connect. He took it with him when he walked out. And every day it reminded him what a jerk he'd been.

As the day of impact got closer, people panicked, looted, shot each other, committed suicide, knifed each other, cried, screamed, turned to religion, or went insane. Many people, whether by choice or necessity, couldn't get out of the area. One morning on his walk, Tanner saw a body in the lake. He called 9-1-1, but no one came. He guessed they had bigger fish to fry than some poor slob who'd decided to end it all. It got so Tanner saw a different body in the lake every day. He stopped walking on the path by the lake.

One delay or another seemed to interfere with Tanner's own escape. Papers had to be gone through and collected, mortgage forms and statements and the like. He withdrew all his savings and cashed in his stocks. He had lots of stuff and only so much room in the car. And then there were the books—deciding which ones to leave behind was time-consuming. He was uprooting his whole life, right? It was hard.

When the day before impact came, Tanner wanted to take a last walk in the park. Maybe he'd see the rabbit and get to smile. His belongings were finally in the car, the gas tank full. Tanner made the walk short, and then he sat on the boulders and looked at the clear, cloudless sky. His heart was aching and heavy. His blood pressure was probably off the charts.

The rabbit didn't know. While Tanner sat, checking the time but reluctant to move, the rabbit came out of its hole, ate, hopped, went back in, and then did it all again. Tanner had heard that animals could sense impending disasters, but this little guy had no clue. It munched grass and wiggled its nose, just like always.

But Tanner's heart didn't lighten. He didn't smile. Because he knew what he was going to do.

He was going to save this rabbit.

Tanner sized up the boulder. It seemed manageable yet big enough to do the job. When he picked it up, his back protested. But that was okay. It wouldn't be much longer. Then he waited for the rabbit to come out one last time. For a moment, sirens sounded close, up the hill on the road. A few screams too. Then they faded.

Tanner would make it quick. The rabbit wouldn't suffer. Not the nuclear winter, not the acid rain, not the shortage of food or water. It wouldn't linger through the burning, insufferable lack of oxygen. Tanner would do the job and then he'd run like he did in high school back to his car and get the hell on the road.

They say things get easier the more you rehearse them in your mind. Tanner rehearsed it over and over, and it didn't get easier. But what else could he do? He stood holding the boulder, listening to the birds. He cried great hitching, grunting sobs that hurt his stomach. No one came along the trail. They were too busy waiting to die or running from disaster.

Then the birds stopped. The horizon darkened. There was a curious high crackling. Tanner realized one asteroid had thumbed its nose at 90 percent and gotten a jump on things. Breaking to pieces in the atmosphere, it rained down hulking, smoking fireballs the size of houses, the size of cars, the size of golf balls, the size of peas.

Tanner watched the rabbit come out of its hole. He raised the boulder chest high, his arms shaking. The rabbit found a blade of grass and nibbled it free, slid it between its lips and chewed. The blade of grass trembled as it ate.

Tanner trembled too. He took a deep breath. It had to be now.

The rabbit finally realized something was wrong. It jerked to and fro, nervous. Its wise brown eyes shone as it looked for the cause of its unease.

Then its eyes turned to Tanner's, and he saw red, fiery doom reflected in them. The sky was thundering, bloody and burning. The pressure in Tanner's ears and face was unbearable. The rabbit froze, crouched low to the ground.

The blunted blade of grass dropped unfinished.

With a cry, Tanner flung the boulder sideways, away.

He slid to the ground beside the rabbit, covering it with his body instead. It didn't move as he cradled it. Its fur was the softest thing he'd ever touched. Its little heart fluttered against his pounding one. Its nose twitched. Tanner breathed against the warm, translucent skin of its delicate ears.

They both calmed. They stopped trembling. Their breathing synced, slow and even.

And then the ground shattered in blazing pieces all around.

MAZE

I.

A baby is crying.

Red neon splashes through the window of the semidark room. Maze sits up in bed and snaps on a lamp. She might have been happy once, and beautiful...but at twenty-nine years old, she has a haunted expression. The dim bulb reveals a stark one-room apartment: gray walls, beat-up furniture. Tidy, but there's no money here.

Maze goes to Frankie, her two-year-old boy, who stands in his crib sniffling. She picks him up, cooing and murmuring. "Shh, baby," she says. "Shh." He stops crying.

Her phone rings. Holding the baby, Maze searches through rumpled bedclothes and finds the phone. It's coiled and fits around her wrist with shape memory. She puts it to her ear. She is expressionless.

"You have three problems to handle tonight." The same male, monotone voice she's heard for the past three years.

"All right," she replies, as always. She doesn't dare refuse.

"Go to your facility to learn about your first problem. After you solve it, you will learn about the others."

"All right."

"That's all."

She needs to know. "Wait—I was told..."

A pause. Maze holds her breath.

Then: "Told?"

"That these would be the last problems I need to solve," she says. "Then I'm done."

Another pause. "You are correct."

Maze allows herself a hopeful smile.

"That's all," the voice says.

"Wait—how—"

Click.

Maze, in the hallway with the baby, knocks on the door to another apartment. Next to her a stain smears the wall—blood or shit, it's hard to tell. The sound of many locks being unlocked, then the door opens. Mrs. Brown, hardened by seventy years of adversity, peers out. She doesn't have a lot of teeth.

"Mrs. Brown, hi, there's been another emergency at the hospital."

Mrs. Brown tiredly takes the baby. She's done this many times. Maze gives the old woman a handful of crumpled dollar bills.

"Last time there was two men." Mrs. Brown nods down the hallway.

Alarmed: "While I was gone?"

"They hung around, then they left. They didn't look right."

"That won't happen anymore, Mrs. Brown, I promise.

I'm quitting my job after tonight."

"You shouldn't. Nurses are in short supply."

"But I have to think about Frankie." Maze gives her little boy a goodnight kiss.

Mrs. Brown takes Frankie into her apartment and closes the door.

On the street, moonlight struggles through rusty smog. Garbage blows across the deserted asphalt. Most buildings are half-collapsed, windows shattered. Two ragged little kids wander up the street pulling a red wagon piled with useful trash: metal, clothes, dead rats.

A broken-down bar on the corner, neon sign sputtering, pounds out disharmonic music. A few rough types stand outside shooting up with something. Maze carries herself like a badass, and they know to leave her alone.

The sign at the back door of the morgue says 'Delivery.' The place is deserted, walls covered in graffiti. Maze pulls on the rusted door. It groans open.

No light. Maze feels her way past dented metal slabs, comes to a wall of drawers for bodies. She opens a drawer.

The first thing she pulls out: night-vision glasses. She slips them on. She pulls out a laser pistol, checks the clip, tucks it in her jeans. She pulls out a photo of a condo building with an address. She pulls out a cardkey.

Back on the empty street, the night-vision glasses tinge everything grayish. Large video screens on every corner, imprinted with the logo 'Nation,' are dead or show static.

Maze hurries past them, intent on her mission.

The wall is made of cheap cement with barbed wire on top. Inside the wall are better buildings, cleaner streets. Their corner video screens are on, showing advertisements. A few residents are out walking, shopping. They even smile.

Two guards patrol near the wall, and drones buzz overhead, but Maze stays in the shadows. She skillfully climbs up, finding cracks to use as hand- and footholds, shimmies under the barbed wire, and drops silently on the other side.

In the residential section, most of the condos are unlit, empty. Maze finds the right building and uses her cardkey to slip through the double front doors. The lobby is dim and empty, but clean. Maze makes her way soundlessly across the tile floor. Footsteps clack from around the corner. Maze hurries to the elevators. A stainless-steel door groans slowly open. She steps in.

The door doesn't move. Maze frantically presses the button. Another groan, and the door finally lurches and slides. The footsteps are faster, nearer—

Maze clenches her teeth. "Come on!"

The door grinds closed. The elevator heaves upward.

When the elevator opens, there's a clean corridor with mood lighting, a contrast to her filthy building. Maze finds the correct door and listens a beat, then uses the cardkey.

She moves fast through the dark condo. In the gray-tinged light of her glasses, she notices nice things, plants, works of art.

Erik Kellar, bland and balding at fifty, rouses from the couch. "Who are—? Street trash? Who let you in? Get out!"

Maze raises the gun, aims—

Kellar fumbles for a weapon, aims back—

Maze pulls the trigger, the shot half-bullet, half-laser—

It misses as Kellar dives to the floor, rolls—

He fires back—

Maze dodges and fires again—

Kellar collapses, bleeding. "Please..." He looks at her.

She never knows the right words. "It's my job." She fires a last time so he doesn't suffer. Frenzied knocks on the door. "Mr. Kellar? Mr. Kellar!"

Maze darts out glass doors to the balcony, leaps at a tree, grabs for a branch, almost misses—

Clumsily swings, then slides down—

And hits the ground running.

She stays in the shadows, moving quickly. A siren starts somewhere and gets louder. A bedraggled woman appears beside Maze, shoves a flyer in her hand, then ducks away into the night.

Maze reads it: 'Robo's Diner. Specials Daily. Open All Night.'

—

The library's stone façade is blown off, books and shelves tipped and scattered. A lion statue out front is missing its head. Murphy, thirty-year-old boyish good looks and nerd glasses covering a sarcastic edge, sits on the statue playing a videogame on an old Nintendo 3DS system.

Two burly men in militaristic uniforms approach and regard Murphy warily. "Are you the, uh, Eggman?" the first one asks.

Murphy looks up. "No, I'm the Walrus. Goo goo ga joob."

"Huh?"

The second one tries. "Which one is the Eggman?"

"Actually, Sam I Am is the Eggman," Murphy says. "He's made of green ham. And the Walrus was Paul."

"What are you talking—?"

"Losers." Murphy grins and hops off the lion. "The passphrase was 'We are the Eggmen, you are the Walrus.' Now how do I know you're legit?"

The first burly man turns red in the face. "Just show us the goods."

Inside the library, four duffel bags are stacked on a scorched table. Murphy opens a bag, pulls out two more Nintendo 3DS videogame systems, and hands them to the burly men.

"Sweet," the second burly man says.

The first one asks, "This all of them? The remotes?"

Murphy nods. "Work from anywhere. Just press this button. Batteries are solar." He grins. "What're you planning on remotely doing?"

The first burly man shoves Murphy against the wall.

"None of your damn business."

He pushes a wad of cash into Murphy's hands, then helps the second man grab the four duffel bags. They stride away.

Murphy's eyes narrow dangerously. He wanders down a still-intact aisle, browsing books. He picks out a wrinkled paperback—Golding's *Lord of the Flies*. He puts it in his pocket.

—

Maze, sans glasses, steps cautiously through the door of Robo's Diner. A scruffy man in a booth slumps over a plate of hash. The waitress smokes a cigarette and watches the big-screen TV above the counter.

Maze sits at the counter and tips up a white cup. The waitress pours coffee.

On the TV, Anders Woo, at forty all handsome, all politician, is in the middle of a speech. Under his image it reads 'Interim Nation Leader Anders Woo.'

"Two wars," Woo croons. "Three if you count that little skirmish in Montana. Bankruptcy. And recovery. Some call it a bailout. Some call it selling out and turning into just another mega corporation." He fixes the camera with his intense gaze. "I don't abide that kind of talk. Look around, and be proud. When have we not had strife, had challenges? And we are still here. We are Nation."

'Nation: Support Our Sponsors' and 'Nation: Rebuilding' scrolls at the bottom of the screen. Canned applause comes from the TV.

Woo continues. "If I'm elected, the Rebuilding of Nation will be my first priority. It's up to you and—"

He's interrupted by an assistant whispering in his ear. Then abruptly, a newscaster comes on. Live footage shows the condo where Maze was earlier, now surrounded by solar vehicles with flashing lights.

"Police aren't saying yet if they have any leads in a brutal shooting that happened only an hour ago. A security guard found the body of Erik Kellar at his home in Nation's Third Zone. Kellar is one of three candidates for president in this historical first election since the end of the wars..."

Maze almost spills her coffee. Her eyes are wide, riveted to the screen.

On the TV, Woo, appearing shaken and solemn, addresses the camera again. "This is a travesty. We will find you, do you hear? We will find you."

An off-camera interviewer's voice: "Are you going ahead with your campaign, Leader Woo?"

"You bet we will," he affirms. "Erik might have been my opponent, but he was a good man, and I know he'd want us to keep going for the good of Nation."

The scruffy man in the diner booth snorts, makes an obscene gesture at the TV. A scar runs across one of his cheeks and down his neck. His voice is raspy. "Yeah, careful the rats don't win. There's more'a us than you!"

Now on the TV there's live footage of reporters

following presidential candidate Tucker Downey, down-to-earth at fifty-five, not slick like Woo but still a politician.

"...I extend my deepest sympathies to his family."

The same reporter's offscreen voice: "Do you think the killer is targeting this year's candidates in the Nation campaign?"

"If so, he'll find we don't run scared around these parts." Downey gives a greasy smile.

In the diner, the scruffy man is up and lurching toward the front door. He mutters as he passes Maze. "You're both dead meat, ya don't watch out..." He goes out the door.

It takes a beat for Maze to register what the scruffy man said. She rushes after him.

But he's disappeared into the night. Maze weaves through pedestrians, searching. She gives up and ducks into an alley, frantically dials her phone.

"These are important people!" she shouts into it. "The next president?"

"Don't ever call this number." The monotone voice.

Maze is pissed. "Look, I've always done your dirty work. I've been your whipped little assassin and never questioned. But this is crazy land. Now you want me to do the other two, right? Right?"

"You have until morning to handle your remaining problems. That's all."

Click.

On every corner the big video screens show political

advertisements. What few solar cars and buses there are also have video screens. Tickers scroll 'Nation: Tear Down to Rebuild' and 'Nation: You Can Decide' and 'New Nation, New World.'

Maze walks until Nation Headquarters looms, a ten-story black building with tinted windows in the middle of a concrete square. A dead fountain of stagnant water is out front. A crumbling stone arch stands at one end of the square.

Hologram posters of Anders Woo and Tucker Downey adorn the entrance. On a third hologram poster, Erik Kellar's face is superimposed with a bouquet of white flowers.

Guards wearing militaristic uniforms and carrying laser rifles patrol outside. Maze watches from the shadows, studying their movements. She counts two dozen guards before turning away.

She makes her way back over the wall to the squalor of her side—

Then has to duck out of sight when she almost stumbles on two workers fixing a video screen. The screen flickers, shows snow, flickers again. Then there's a political ad of an ever-smiling Anders Woo.

In a cobblestoned alley near her apartment, Maze picks her way through broken glass, garbage, human bones. A homeless woman sprawls in the alley. She's thin, eyes rolled up, e-needle in her arm. Attached to a leash on her wrist is a dirty-faced six-year-old girl. The little girl reaches a hopeful hand toward Maze.

Maze pauses in midstride. "Sorry I don't have anything for you, sweetie."

Maze's phone rings a peculiar series of tones. She listens, then heads down the street.

The metal detector in front of the corner grocer is for customers. A short but muscular bouncer collects every customer's weapon—guns, pipes, knives. Maze gives her gun to the man and goes in.

Cramped shelves of boxed and canned food, bins of limp vegetables, bottles of water. Maze makes her way through narrow aisles to a back room.

Here it's clean, spare. She kneels to pet Rowdy, a furry, friendly dog. A faded photograph is pinned to the wall, a group of soldiers posing with their guns, Maze among them.

An enormous smiling man in a motorized chair, Harry, baby-faced at forty-five, rolls forward to greet her. A slimmer Harry was posing next to Maze in the photo.

"How's Rowdy the bomb-sniffing genius?" she asks.

"The only bombs he's been sniffing lately are his own farts," Harry says wryly. "I get to sniff them too, which is more than I signed up for."

"How are you, Harry? Still saving the world one stew can at a time?"

"You should try it sometime. It's good for the soul."

Now to business. "Got your signal," she says.

"You had a delivery." Harry nods at a thick envelope on a table.

Maze picks it up, hesitates. "Did you see who delivered it?"

"Didn't see. Don't want to know. I'm just a waystation."

Maze opens the envelope. Stacks of money fall out, along with a note. "This is huge, Harry. Bigger than anything they've had me do before. It's not good." She gives Harry the money. "Maybe I should go after them instead, huh?"

"Sure, if you could find them." He holds the money back out to her. "Take some of this."

She shrugs and takes a stack. Harry rolls his chair over to a bed and stuffs the rest under the mattress. Maze reads the note, the special paper disintegrating fast in her fingers.

He says, "If you went after them, hell, if you deviated from what they told you, they'd torture you. Kill you. You know that, right?"

"So?"

"They'd do the same to your little boy."

Maze pulls something else from the envelope—a slinky black dress, barely a handful of fabric.

Soon Maze, in the slinky black dress and carrying a box, walks through the alley toward the homeless woman and little girl. They watch as Maze sets down the box of food and water. Maze touches the little girl's hand, gives her a smile, and then disappears into the night.

A solar van is parked at the back entrance of a rundown hotel. Two teenage girls, probably underage but it's hard to tell beneath all their face and body makeup, stand waiting, cold, bored. Maze slips from a corner of the building and approaches. She holds up her stack of money. The girls look at each other. One nods, and then the other one. One takes the cash and ambles away.

"What's your name?" Maze asks the other one.

"Here I don't have a name," the girl replies. She's pretty, with long black hair. Her voice is young.

A slick assistant in dark glasses comes out the back door. He hesitates and squints at Maze. The girl takes Maze's hand and says, "She's my sister." The assistant shrugs and motions to them to follow him. Maze gives the girl's hand a grateful squeeze.

They go inside the back door, and then into an elevator. When they reach their floor, the assistant leads them out of the elevator and down the hall. The assistant knocks on the door to Room 713. It opens.

Maze follows the girl in. The assistant closes the door behind them. A man with a greasy smile comes forward: Tucker Downey, presidential candidate.

Downey pours himself a glass of expensive whiskey. He's already very drunk. "Have a seat," he says.

Maze, watching Downey with narrowed eyes, sits next to the girl on a couch.

"I'm an important man," Downey says. "I work for

Nation, and that means I work for the people. Even you girls, on this side of the wall. In the destruction. In the filth." He takes a long drink. "Don't worry. If they let me become president, I'll try to be fair to everybody. I really will. But you have to do your part."

He starts filling two cups on a tray with dark liquid.

"What's that?" Maze murmurs to the girl.

"It tastes sweet. You just drink it. Then you go to sleep. He likes to pretend we're dead and then do stuff."

"What stuff?"

"I'm not sure. But it only takes a few hours. Then we leave."

Maze arches a dubious eyebrow.

"Only a few girls have died for real," the girl adds.

Downey approaches Maze and the girl. "Ever heard that expression, you scratch my back, I scratch yours?"

"Uh-huh," the girl answers, taking a cup and drinking the dark liquid.

Maze watches. The girl's eyes roll back in her head. She slides to the floor with a thunk. She looks dead.

Downey nods at the tray and then at Maze. "Come on, darlin'. Don't waste my time."

Maze forces a flirty smile. "Wonder if a girl can get a real drink first. Been a hell of a night so far."

"Has it now..."

Maze stands, moves her body suggestively, walks toward the bar. "Fix me a fancy drink, Mister President?"

Maze asks. "Then maybe I'll give you a scratch."

Downey chuckles and goes to the bar. He's charmed by her. "Well, I'm not president yet."

"I'll vote for you."

He gives her a whiskey, then puts a hand on her, stroking. She downs the drink.

"That turn you on? That I'm such a powerful man?" Downey asks.

"Not in the slightest," Maze replies. She breaks the glass against a table and shoves the jagged edge at Downey's throat—

Downey yells, tries to duck but not in time—

Blood gushes from his throat—

He grabs at Maze, choking—

She twists away as the door bursts open—

The assistant runs in, shooting—

Maze leaps at the assistant's gun—

They roll on the floor—

Maze still has the jagged glass—

She slashes it at the assistant's face as he screams—

Then she jumps to her feet and runs out the door.

Maze barrels down the hall, flings open the door to the stairs. Her hand is cut; she holds it as she hurls herself down each flight. Blood spatters in her wake. Her legs feel sluggish. She's gasping for air. She looks down. The front of her dress has a dark spreading stain. She pokes a finger in a bullet hole. Her finger comes out red.

She stumbles down the stairs to the second landing, almost falls, steadies herself. A second assistant bursts through the door. He's surprised she's right there. He gropes for his gun—

She kicks at his hand—

The gun clatters away—

He and Maze both leap for it—

She's faster, gets it, twists, shoots—

He drops. She continues down the stairs—

Finally, the emergency exit. She falls out the door to the ground, then drags herself to her feet. Sirens start far away, get closer, louder. Maze grabs onto a dumpster. Her hands are shaking.

She roots in the dumpster, finds used duct tape, wraps her bleeding hand. She pulls out a clump of plastic bags, cinches them around her waist as a bandage. The sirens shriek, almost there. She takes off down the street, jogging carefully along, avoiding streetlights or people.

She stops to rest in an alley. A man dressed in black approaches her with a package, sees her condition, falters. He's unsure.

"Do you have instructions for me?" Maze asks.

The thwak-thwak sound of a quadcopter, black, insectlike, sleek—a Cop Copter. Its search beams sweep the area.

The man shakes his head and ducks back into the shadows.

"Wait! I'm okay. Give me the— Dammit!"

The search beam almost finds her. She dodges out of the way while the Copter crosses overhead. She sees the man in black hurry toward the city park. She chases after.

She jogs through the gate. Benches and heaps of garbage are made into shelters. Trashcan fires reveal dirty faces and hungry eyes of the people living here. More Cop Copters, distant. Maze walks carefully, getting stares. She whirls, looks around—the man in black has disappeared.

Near a fountain, a half-dozen feral teenagers, scarred and vicious looking, armed with chains and clubs, leer at Maze. The leader, Crux, a lanky eighteen-year-old, steps in front of her. "What the hell," he says.

Maze stops, wary. "Just passing through."

"Give us your gun. And your boots."

"No."

The other teens laugh. Crux grins, showing teeth filed to points. One of the Cop Copters gets louder, closer.

"Guess we're taking them," he says.

"Try." She brings up her gun.

The teens hesitate. Then blood spatters the ground from under the plastic on Maze's waist. Maze looks down, alarmed.

The teens surge forward to get her. Maze ducks and shoots. Crux leaps, but Maze recoils, cracks the gun upside his head. Another teen clips her arm with his chain. Maze staggers back. They start to overpower her—

The blinding searchlight of a Cop Copter engulfs them. The thwak-thwak of the blades is thunderous as it tilts almost on top of them. Laser bullets rip across the ground. The teens scatter. Some fall. Maze dives through bushes, dodges, runs as searchlights chase her—

More bullets from the Copter tear through. The searchlights reflect off garbage piles and shelters. People scream in panic.

Maze races out the park gates, the Copter almost on top of her—

She reaches into her boot, feeling around—

Pulls out a thumb-sized electronic device—

Attaches it to her gun—

And flings the gun up at the Copter—

Where it lodges in the landing gear.

Maze heads at a staggering run the other way—

As the landing gear explodes.

The Copter, in flames, careens slantways, engine shrieking—

And crashes in a heap in the trees.

Maze keeps running.

Finally, she has to stop. It's dark, quiet. Near a staticky Nation video screen, she pulls back the plastic to look at her stomach. Some blood spills out. She's bad. She forces herself to keep calm. She takes a deep breath and re-ties the plastic as tight as she can, wincing.

Behind her, the video screen sputters to life, and Maze

is on it. In real time. She's silhouetted against the backdrop of her bigger video image, both moving in unison.

Maze hears the sound of her own gasps coming from the speakers.

She whirls—

—

Messy desks, coffee cups, half-eaten donuts. But these cops use wireless headsets and holographic 3-D computers. Trilla, an efficient thirty-year-old in a crisp shirt, hair tight in a ponytail, leans eagerly over her touchpad computer. On-screen is Maze—now realizing she's on video and starting to run again.

"Got her, Captain," Trilla says into her headset. "She's hooked."

In his office piled with books and papers instead of electronics, Captain Jayks, five o'clock shadow on his middle-aged, craggy face, yells into a videophone.

"She crashed one of our Copters! And that's on— No, that's on your head!" He's exasperated. "I have to go." He fumbles with his headset. "Thanks, Trilla. Put her on."

In the squadroom, a half-dozen cops stand around a table now showing a holographic image of Maze. Trilla attaches pads to her fingers, sweeps her hand in the air to control the 3-D image and sound. Jayks joins them.

In the holographic image, Maze stumbles along a dark street, one hand pressed to her stomach. Around her, video screens sputter to life, showing her, or if they're already on, switching to her channel. The angle jerks and changes every little bit as she moves out of range of one video screen and into another.

Trilla zooms in. Jayks studies Maze intently.

A crackle, and the image goes dead. Trilla tilts her hand, moves her fingers. "Signal keeps fading," she says. "I'll get Satellite on it."

The image sputters on again. Then off. Then on.

Jayks pokes at the touchpad, says, "How about this—?" The image goes dead.

Trilla gives Jayks a look. He backs off. She gets the image on again. She sweeps her hand. Stats about Maze scroll across her image—description, location, history.

—

On the street, Maze rounds a corner to a darker area. She dials her phone. "Come on... Hello! Mrs. Brown?"

In Mrs. Brown's apartment, the wallpaper is stained, peeling. And she's a hoarder—papers and gray junk are piled everywhere. Mrs. Brown sits on a threadbare couch, blanket around her. Frankie sleeps next to her.

Mrs. Brown, cranky, sleepy, answers the phone. "What is it? Are you still at the hospital?"

Maze is in a hurry. "Is Frankie okay?"

"He's sleeping. Want me to wake him up?"

"No, but...but when he does, can you tell him—"

A knock at Mrs. Brown's door. Irritated, the old woman gets her bulk off the couch, makes her way across the dim room. She yells at the door. "Who is it?"

Maze, in the phone: "What's going on?"

"Someone's at the door."

Maze is suddenly scared. "Don't let them in. Mrs. Brown?" There's no answer. "Mrs. Brown? Don't let them in! Hello?"

The line has gone dead. There's the sound of distant Cop Copters. Down the street, a staticky video screen buzzes to life with Maze's image. Maze stifles a sob, holds her stomach, and heads away at a painful lope.

The waterfront. Dirty wisps of fog trail across the oily water. A buoy clangs from somewhere. Maze stops again and dials her phone. "I know you told me not to call—" A high-pitched buzz comes from the earpiece. She clicks off, then dials again. "I'll do what you want! Just give me some help. You don't have to take my baby—"

The buzz comes again. She clicks off, defeated. She leans against the railing.

She looks down at the dark water.

Behind her, a low growl. She whirls—

Two snarling, clacking, robotic Catatrons, big as ponies, slink out of the dark. Metallic slicing blades for teeth, green tracking lights for eyes, razor claws at the ends of four articulated legs—they're hunting-and-killing machines.

Maze, stunned, desperate, looks for escape. There are abandoned buildings on the boardwalk. Not far. She just has to get there.

Ripping her phone from her wrist, she taps the screen and then tosses it as far as she can. It plays tinny music as it flies. The Catatrons, metal ears perked, track it with their electronic eyes, take a few steps in its direction.

Maze doesn't wait. She's off at a dead run toward the boardwalk.

———

Trilla tries to get a better picture of the 3-D image. Every angle is grainy and dark.

Jayks motions to the other officers. "She's as locked as you're gonna get."

They nod and head out the door with weapons.

"She's out of visual range," Trilla says.

"Switch to Cat cam."

Trilla waves her hand. The image switches to two scratchy infrared visuals from both Catatrons' cameras.

———

On the boardwalk, burned out, blackened buildings with faded billboards are all that's left. Wooden planks of the rotted walkway. A giant white clown face looms out of the darkness, the entrance to the Funhouse. Half its face is burned away, red lips scorched, grinning teeth now splintered fangs.

Maze barrels toward the open-mouth doorway of the Funhouse.

Inside, arcade games are tipped and smashed. Giant stuffed animals are dismembered, scorched, stuffing hanging out. Maze turns to see the Catatrons burst through the clown-mouth doorway—

She tosses stuffed animal parts toward them, then runs—

The Catatrons leap and snap, tossing the parts aside—

Maze makes it into the Labyrinth of Mirrors. She catches little reflections of herself in jagged shards. Her boots crunch on splintered glass.

The snarling Catatrons are almost there—

She hangs a quick left down a twisted corridor, loses the Catatrons for a brief moment—

Then they're back on her heels—

Another fork in the corridor—

Maze dodges down the left one—

One Catatron follows her. The other takes the right.

As the corridors meet again, Maze is trapped like a mouse—

Maze jumps, tries to duck past—

The Catatrons both twist and lunge toward her—

One razored claw catches her thigh—

Maze tumbles to the floor, bleeding, rolling into—

A round, all-mirrored room, surprisingly intact. A hundred reflections of herself cascade toward each other—

One of the Catatrons follows, going for her throat—

Maze knows she's dead—

Then watches in amazement as that Catatron stops up short—

And the other one charges past to ram headlong into one of her reflections—

Glass erupts—

The Catatrons, confused by hers and their endless reflections, charge every which way, snapping, jerking, haphazard.

—

A chaos of holographic images. Jayks and Trilla can't make anything out. Trilla tries adjustments.

Jayks mutters, "Damn technology..."

—

Maze makes it to her feet, stumbles away from the snarling chaos—

She limps hurriedly out the back door of the Funhouse to the waterfront. The foggy river churns a few feet away. A buoy clangs again.

She notices in the darkness a pulsing red light coming from her wound—

A tracker slug.

"Hell."

No time to address it right now. She clambers down a metal stairwell to the dock, stops at rusted drums of leaking fuel—

The Catatrons appear on the stairs, eagerly rush down—

Maze pulls another thumb-sized device from her boot—

Tosses the device into one of the drums—
Then jumps over the side of the dock—
To land painfully in a small rowboat.

The dock explodes—

Maze grabs on as the force of the blast flings the boat in the air—

It splashes down in the middle of the river. Maze winces and sits up.

The fuel drums on the dock sink amid roaring, flaming wreckage. The Catatrons are nowhere to be seen.

—

The holographic image goes to static. Trilla waves her padded fingers but can't get the picture back.

"We're out," she says.

—

Maze catches her breath. She pokes at the red, pulsing bullet hole, gasps in pain. Then, to her horror, she sees something happening on what's left of the dock.

Scorched, half-melted, the Catatrons yowl and snarl as they leap at each other, grind together, their nanotechnology altering, meshing, combining...to become one bigger, badder Giant Catatron.

Half its body is blackened, melted, one tracking-light eye sputtering. It drags a metal paw. The Giant Catatron, big as a rhinoceros, sticks a tentative metallic claw in the water, testing.

Then it jumps into the river and swims for Maze's boat.

Maze frantically finds one oar and starts paddling. The current is fast here. The boat moves downriver.

But the Giant Catatron is faster—

Soon it splashes beside the boat—

Scrabbles and claws, trying to hoist itself in—

Maze beats it with the oar. It roars, clinging to the side of the boat.

Nearby, giant slabs of concrete and metal debris jut out of the water. Maze desperately paddles toward them. The Giant Catatron's jaws clamp on the oar, break it in half—

The boat jerks and twists, catches on debris—

Maze is thrown to the floor of the boat—

The Giant Catatron scrambles in—

The boat tips—

Maze tumbles onto the debris and grabs on—

As the Giant Catatron and the boat are pulled away by the current…

Gasping for breath, Maze finds a scrap of rebar, tests the sharpness of the end. She rips open the plastic around her waist—

Takes a deep breath—

"Okay," she mutters. "Okay. See the ball, be the ball. See the ball… Be. The ball."

She digs the end of the rebar into the bullet hole—

Cries out, doubled over in pain—

As her fingers find the red pulsing bullet and pull it out.

Water surges nearby—

Electronic snarling and scrambling—
The Giant Catatron hoists itself onto the debris—
Its tracking eye locks onto her—
Maze holds up the bullet—
Then throws it as far as she can out into the water.
The Giant Catatron freezes, tracking eye sputtering—
Then it splashes back into the water after the bullet.
The noises get fainter—
And then are gone.

Maze, weak, faint, fumbles with the blood-soaked plastic, tightens it.

—

Harry's corner grocer. She's made it this far, but the doors are chained, the place dark. From her alley vantage point, Maze sags, defeated, against the brick wall.

Footsteps in the alley. Maze summons one more scrap of strength and wields her rebar, ready to fight. Murphy comes around the corner, then stops up short.

"Whoa, easy. Just on my way to Harry's for raisin bran."

"Closed."

"Really? They're never closed." Murphy stares at her, curious.

Maze, squinting, suspicious: "And nobody's had boxed cereal for years."

"You'd be amazed at what underground trading can get you."

Maze is too weak from loss of blood. "But..." She slides

onto her butt, feebly holding up her rebar weapon. Then she passes out.

II.

Dreamy, dim lights. Maze, half-conscious, sees things only in fragments. It's an apartment. Murphy approaches the bed with bandages, sits next to her. Murphy plays guitar—quite well—and sings—quite badly. Murphy makes coffee at the stove.

Then Maze is really dreaming, and there's a field of tall grass and colorful flowers. She leads Frankie by the hand. A butterfly hovers near his head, making him giggle. Maze's smile is full of love. Then the hovering butterfly darts away in panic. Maze turns in the tall grass to see Frankie is suddenly gone.

"Frankie? Frankie? Frankie!"

The loud thwak-thwak of a Cop Copter sweeps overhead, then fades. Gray light comes from a tiny window. The cramped studio apartment is full of dusty old computers, electronics, game consoles, and stacks and stacks of video games.

Murphy plays *Fallout 3* with the sound low. In the game on the TV screen, cities lay in twisted, gray ruin.

Maze wakes up. She sees it's morning and stumbles out of bed, confused, all adrenaline. "No...no..."

Murphy tries to calm her. "It's okay, you're gonna be—"

"What time is it? Is it really—? Oh, God, they've got

him." She's weak but determined. She heads to the door, but Murphy blocks her.

"Got who? Hey, calm down. The only gluestitch I could find was way past its expiration."

Maze pulls back the bandages on her stomach. A bumpy, gooey but effective line covers her now closed wound. She staggers a little, dizzy.

"It's still drying," he says. "You better sit down. You lost a lot of blood."

She slides to a chair. "Can I borrow your phone?"

Murphy hands her a phone. She dials fast. It just rings. She dials again. Just the high-pitched buzz from before. She clicks off. She eyes Murphy suspiciously. He brings over a mug of coffee.

"Here."

She takes the mug, sniffs its contents. She doesn't drink as she looks around the room. "Who do you work for? Do you work for Nation?"

"I don't work for anybody," Murphy replies. "I guess for myself. I trade."

"What do you trade?"

"Mostly batteries, electronics, generators. Some other stuff."

"Guns?"

"Not guns. Sorry." He's fidgety under her suspicious stare. He goes over to her boots by the bed. "These are pretty sweet, though. What do you want for them?"

In a flash she's up and behind Murphy. As he turns, she throws the coffee in his face, kicks his legs from under him. Murphy goes down hard. In one swift motion, Maze plants her knees on his arms, grabs one of her boots, and points the sharp heel near Murphy's eye.

"Don't tell me you have all this equipment," she says, "that you're a trader, but you don't keep a gun. Where is it?"

He's still calm, good-humored. "I said I don't trade guns, not that I don't have one. You just had to ask."

Maze eyes him. "You trust me with a gun."

"Well, if you were gonna kill me, I'd be dead by now, right?"

"You still could be." But she lets him up.

He wipes coffee from his face. "Where did you learn to do that?"

"In the army. Special Forces..." Now something's caught her eye. TV monitors show real-time feeds of different parts of the city. "Do you spy on people?"

"Uh... Well..."

"You hacked into Nation's network?"

Murphy's reluctant. "I...sort of do surveillance for some of my customers. It's hard to explain, but basically—"

"Can you get a feed of my apartment building?" she asks. Her eyes are bright with excitement.

"It's only possible if there are camera screens, if you're on the watch list. And if Nation doesn't want you to know you're being watched, finding those screens—"

"Believe me. I'm being watched."

He shrugs, sits at a dusty keyboard, and starts typing. "You've actually been splashed across the airwaves all night."

To illustrate, Murphy pulls up earlier footage of her running. Her biographical data ticks on the screen.

Maze leans closer and watches him work. She notices her proximity makes him both nervous and thrilled.

"Why are you helping me?" she asks. "If you turned me in, Nation would give you a sweet reward."

Murphy chuckles. "If Nation knew about me, my head would be stuck up on a pike right next to yours."

A live feed of her apartment corridor pops up. At the far end, Mrs. Brown's door is open.

"There. Zoom in."

Murphy zooms the camera in. Mrs. Brown's lifeless body lies in the doorway. There's no sign of Frankie.

Maze's expression is murderous. "Can you play the footage from late last night?"

Murphy brings up the night's footage and rewinds, finds what she needs.

On-screen, two men with guns knock on Mrs. Brown's door. A moment later the door opens. It's over in seconds. One man shoots the old woman while the other goes into the apartment. He comes out holding Frankie by the waist. The little boy struggles. They disappear out of frame, leaving Mrs. Brown dying on the floor.

Maze moans, stumbles away, and retches. She fights not to cry.

—

Captain Jayks pokes around the corner grocer's backroom among Harry's meager belongings. Jayks finds an electric razor, turns it on. Its buzzing motor cuts in and out. He tries it on his face.

Trilla sticks her head in. "Still nothing on the criminal, Captain. But we're sweeping all sectors."

Jayks motions to her. "Solar batteries don't work worth a damn. Any manual razors out there?"

"Um...I didn't look." She gives the room a perfunctory glance. "Electronic imprint last puts her in an alley across from this store. Then she vanishes."

Jayks puts the razor back. "Hm." He looks around.

"She either blocked her signal, or she altered it. Maybe I can run some DNA algorithms, plug one of those in?"

Jayks pulls the faded photo from the wall—the group of soldiers, Harry and Maze with their arms around each other. "He knows her," he says. "Let's find him." Jayks stoops and then holds up a battered bowl with the faded words '#1 Best Friend' on it. He sniffs it. "He'll have a dog with him."

He sees scrapes on the floor, follows them with his fingers. The scrapes form a well-worn trail of two lines. Jayks puzzles it out, staring at the photo. "He might have a war injury? And be in a chair..."

At Trilla's surprised expression, he shrugs. "Don't overlook good old-fashioned detective work."

Trilla takes the photo and goes to the door. Then she turns, gives the hint of a smile. "Oh, um? I think all the stylish guys these days are going with beards."

Trilla ducks out the door. Jayks runs a thoughtful hand over his rough chin.

—

Maze sits under the tiny window watching a brown bird hop along a ledge outside. It didn't know the world was over; it just kept looking for seeds to eat.

Murphy approaches and sits next to her. "Was that your little boy?" he asks.

Maze nods.

"Who took him?"

"I don't know. Nation. Or someone trying to overthrow Nation. Whoever's had me dangling from their string for the past three years. Because I didn't finish what they told me to do in time."

"I'm sorry," Murphy says. "Sometimes I've thought I wanted kids, ya know? But this world...it's so screwed up. And I can barely take care of myse—"

"Where can I get weapons?"

Murphy blinks. "Uh..."

Maze gets up and, though weak, starts going through Murphy's drawers and closets. "I'll pay you, if that's what you're worried about." She looks down at what remains of her slinky dress. "I'll need clothes too."

"Hey, I saw the news special. Ex-soldier with a grudge tries to take out the new government by killing all the candidates. To your kind, the Rebuild is a joke. You say it's because someone threatened your little boy?"

"And because I'm good at my job."

"Am I missing something?" he asks. "Whoever's been puppet-mastering you just killed your son. Not to mention, you're kind of half-dead yourself."

"There's a chance. Those men killed the old woman, but they took Frankie alive. So there's a chance, and that's what I have to go with."

He gives up and digs through his clothes for something to fit her. "How many weapons are we talking?"

"Enough to get in and out of Nation Headquarters. Preferably alive."

He stops. "Don't tell me you're going after Anders Woo."

"I was given a mission, and if I fulfill it, I just might get my son back. I have to try."

Murphy hands her some clothes. She shucks off what she's wearing. He shyly averts his eyes.

She dresses quickly. "So...weapons?"

"I have a contact. But it won't be easy."

"I can get money—"

"Don't worry about it," he says. "I owe him a trade."

Later, Maze sits on the bed rewrapping her bandages.

Images of her and the political candidates play on the TV news. The sound is off.

Murphy finishes stuffing a backpack with supplies and comes over. "Anything more on the election? Another candidate besides Woo?"

Maze shrugs. "I'm not real political. Anyway, it doesn't matter who wins. The rich will always have the power. And the rest of us will always live like rats. There's no Rebuild going on. Not for people like us."

Murphy gently takes the bandages from her fumbling fingers and wraps her wound. Their faces are close; his arms go around her as he works. He gazes into her eyes.

"Maybe I still have hope," he says.

"Hope is something they sell on TV. But I don't buy it."

He's done. "These should hold. We better get going." His eyes linger on hers.

She knows he wants to kiss her. She gently slides away, then goes to his computer monitors. "There's one more thing maybe you can do."

A few minutes later, Maze watches Murphy at his computer.

"Do you know how many three-hundred-pound neo-hippy ex-soldiers in motorized chairs with dogs there are out there?" He searches a few more seconds. "Okay. This might be him."

The screen shows the scrambled view of someone on the other end.

"You're sure we're secure?" she asks.

"Snug as a bug."

Maze types in the message window: 'Hairy canines make better companions.'

Murphy chuckles. "That's your passphrase?"

"If it's Harry, he'll know the reply."

A beat. Then a reply in the message window: 'Only the dogs, not the teeth. Are you safe???'

Maze smiles, relieved. "It's Harry." She types in the window: 'I'm safe. Are you? And Rowdy?'

A beat. Up pops: 'Rowds and I both OK. Sudden attention on the store. Had to skedaddle.'

Maze types: 'Sorry about that.'

A beat. Then: 'We have to meet. Something big. Need your help.'

"Wonder what that's about," Murphy says.

Maze types: 'I'm there. Stay low. Contact you soon.'

A beat. Then from Harry: 'Soon. Be careful, sweetie. Over and out.'

Maze logs off, somber.

"Something big?" Murphy asks.

"Yeah." She's thoughtful. "Harry's kind of a networker, like you. He's the closest thing I have to family. Except for my son."

"Where's...the father?"

"Dead. Before Frankie was born." Maze cocks her head. "Why are you helping me? Seriously."

"Maybe the world can get better, get livable again. Somebody has to try to make that happen. Why not us?"

It's a hazy dawn. Maze and Murphy make their way through concrete rubble and occasional groups of sleeping people. Maze fiddles with a battery-sized electronic device in her hands. They speak in murmurs.

"This looks like you put it together with sticks and glue," she says.

"Trust me. It scrambles our signal so we're invisible. Unless they start looking for a scrambled signal. In which case, we're toast."

She arches an eyebrow at him, the closest thing she's come to a smile.

Most of the parking garage has collapsed. Gray light filters through the ruins. Maze follows Murphy until they come upon what looks like just another mound of debris. He pulls away rotted boards, bricks, stained tarps—to reveal a small pickup truck.

"I'm impressed," she says.

Murphy grins and checks the solar batteries on the truck, then tosses the backpack in the front seat.

He drives skillfully through the rubble-strewn streets. It's a bad neighborhood, but they see workers in uniforms repairing more video screens.

'Election Tomorrow!' blares across the screens. 'Watch and Vote at Any Screen!'

Maze bites at her lip. "They moved it up."

"Wait. How can there be an election when there's only one candidate?"

"We're cutting it too close."

The sun's stronger at the edge of the city. There's desert sand and scrub, some low buildings and run-down houses, and more rubble. The roads are loaded with rusted husks of cars, long stripped of anything useful.

Murphy carefully drives around a pile-up of a dozen rusted-out cars. Tanned faces of people appear in the broken windows. Some are children. They're living here.

Maze gives them a sad smile.

Murphy pulls the pickup onto the empty highway toward the desert. Maze fiddles with the buttons. Nothing works.

"I've never been to the Null," she says. "Never been out of the city."

Murphy's voice has a new, harder edge. "I vay-cay here every year with Muffy and the kids. It's fabulous."

"How far?"

He hands her a tattered paper map. "If we're fast, we'll be there and back before dark. Don't want to be out here at night."

She studies the map. "What's his name? Your contact?"

"Thrash."

"And Thrash has guns? Weapons?"

"He could probably take out half the city if he wanted."

"Why doesn't he?"

"Then there'd be nobody left to sell guns to."

An hour later, the city is just a skyline behind them. Out here it's desert, with a hot, unforgiving sun. Large flocks of vultures cross the sky. Murphy wipes sweat from his face and drinks water. He hands Maze the metal bottle and she drinks.

She sees something up ahead on the road. "What's that? Stop for a minute."

A lizard as big as a human, mottled brown and red, stretches across the highway, dozing in the sun. Murphy slows the truck and stops, engine running. Maze is about to get out when he puts a hand on her shoulder.

"Does it taste good roasted on a spit?" she asks.

"No. And it's dangerous."

"So am I."

Murphy shakes his head. "I mean really dangerous. Its saliva is venomous. It's fast. It will chase you and eat you. Then again, pretty much everything out here will chase you and eat you."

Maze hesitates, then cautiously opens the truck door a crack. At the sound of the door, the lizard raises its massive head in their direction. Its forked tongue flickers. Its eyes narrow greedily.

Maze quickly closes the door. "What is it?"

"Gila monster. They were a lot smaller before the fallout."

Murphy pulls the truck slowly around the Gila monster,

giving it a wide berth. The big lizard blinks lazily.

The farther they travel outside the city, the worse the highway gets. The truck bounces along in the heat. Finally ahead they see a decrepit three-story office building. What windows aren't broken are gray-tinted. Solar panels cover the roof. The dusty grounds are surrounded by a high fence with barbed wire at the top. Two makeshift guard towers hulk at either corner.

As Murphy's truck approaches the potholed drive, a motorcycle comes up to meet it, driven by a tough-as-nails fifty-year-old in khaki. She carries a laser rifle. The woman peers, unsmiling, into the truck's cab, then motions to Murphy to follow her.

Murphy does so. "That's Rainy, Thrash's wife. She's usually friendly."

"What is this place?" Maze asks.

"Scientists grew organs here. For transplants."

Murphy parks the truck, and he and Maze get out. Rainy gives Murphy a reluctant hug, shooting glances at Maze. Maze watches, on her guard.

"Thrash is inside," Rainy says. "You two thirsty?"

Murphy replies, "Could use a drink. Thanks." He and Maze follow Rainy through the front doors.

Maze murmurs, "Should we watch our backs?"

"Couldn't hurt. But let me do the talking."

The first floor, what used to be the lobby and offices, has been converted into a living area with couches, a huge

TV, posters of musicians on the walls. Laser guns and other weapons are around for easy access in case of trouble. Thrash, gray, spiky hair, leather pants to match his leathery face, and black pointy boots, rises from the couch. He's laid back, with a British accent.

"Hey, Murph, wot's happenin', man."

"How's it going, Thrash?"

The men do fist bumps. Thrash squints, dubious, at Maze. She squints back, equally dubious.

"Who's your chum?"

"She's okay," Murphy says. "She's with me."

Thrash and Rainy exchange glances. "It's just that you always come alone," Thrash says. "It's understood, innit. And this one looks a bit more troubled than I like."

"We won't be any trouble." Murphy digs into his backpack, pulls out a few packets of guitar strings.

Thrash is suddenly less suspicious. "These wot I think they are?" He takes the packets.

"I owed you, remember?"

"Ah, man, this is great." Thrash gives a big grin.

"We're hoping you can hook us up."

Thrash takes another assessment of Maze. "We'll see wot we can do. I'm not promising anyfing." To Maze: "Nofing personal, love."

Maze goes to reply, but Thrash throws his arm around Murphy and steers him eagerly to a couch, where guitars and amps are set up. "Let's fire up these pretty babies and see how they sound. Rainy's concocting amazing things in the kitchen today, and if we're especially melodious, she might share with us..."

Rainy sighs indulgently, smiles, and leads Maze down a hall.

The kitchen is homey, with working appliances. Cases of tequila are stacked in a corner next to cases of grenades and laser rifles. Also a few weapons on the counter at the ready. Rainy goes to a pitcher of margaritas and mashes cactus leaves. Maze looks around, jittery, not able to relax.

"You two came from the city today? That's a long drive." Rainy's voice is now lighter, pleasant.

"Yeah." Maze glances out the back window. There's a garden: ripe tomatoes on vines, corn stalks with ears of corn, tall sunflowers.

"I'm so glad we got out of there," Rainy says. "Not easy making a life here either, but we've got everything we need, you know? You'd be surprised how many settlements are out here now."

"And Nation doesn't bother you?"

"We keep a low profile. Some places are really hidden. We don't make trouble. And we keep visitors to a minimum."

"Sorry."

"No, it's okay. Look, if we can't help each other once in a while, what are we living for? Try this." She gives Maze a slice of cactus to eat. Maze tastes it, finds she likes it.

Two gangly teen boys carrying rifles come in the back door. Maze tenses, almost goes for a weapon. Rainy smiles at the boys, and Maze relaxes a little. The boys grab hunks of bread from a plate, hungrily eat.

"We have customers right now. Why don't you take the rovers and check the perimeter?"

"'Kay, Mom."

"Grab an extra water, please. And here. I got the sand out of these this morning." Rainy hands the boys a couple of laser rifles from the counter. They switch with their dusty ones. They go back out the door. To Maze: "You have kids?"

"One. A little boy."

Loud guitar music comes from the other room. Murphy and Thrash jam on electric guitars. They sound pretty good. Rainy takes in margaritas and gives Thrash a thumbs-up. Thrash grins, playing.

Maze tries to catch Murphy's eye, but he's having a blast, keeping up with the older rocker pretty well. Maze lets her fingers drift over a laser rifle on a table, tries to calm down but she can't. Pissed, she stalks out the door.

She finds a dim stairway, the concrete steps stained. She takes the steps two at a time to the second floor, yanks on a metal door marked Fire Exit. It whines open.

The only light comes from the broken windows. Smashed glass is everywhere—the windows, test tubes, large glass-walled containers. Some containers are intact.

Maze paces the room past the dried-out organs and tissue. Some look familiar—eyeballs, hearts, fingers, toes. Some are just so much jerky-like meat.

A noise, and Maze turns to see Murphy in the doorway. He offers her a margarita. "These are really—" He sees all the body parts. "Wow. Creepy."

She's shaking, barely containing herself. "You do know I'm on a deadline, don't you? I can't screw around like this. Your big trade with him was guitar strings??"

"Hey, they're hard to come by—"

"They have my little boy. God knows what they're doing to him. I just want to break something. I just want to kill something."

"It'll work out. You have to trust me. This is what I do."

"And what are you doing? I could've already—"

"Negotiating. You can't kick and blast your way through here. Thrash would just shoot you and be done with it."

She stares into a glass case of eyeballs, some green with rot. Murphy moves beside her.

He continues, "I'm getting your weapons, okay? Let me do my thing. Let Thrash play his guitar for a while. We'll walk out of here with whatever weapons you need."

A beat. She calms down a little. "It's the only thing I'm good at," she says. "Kicking and blasting. Fighting."

His shoulder touches hers. He bends his head and catches her eye. Softly: "We've all been in survival mode so long we don't know what else to do."

"Did you know I was a nurse for a while in the war? But then they found out I was better at killing."

"Don't you ever get tired of it?"

"I'm tired of it every day." She starts to turn away, but Murphy gently touches her face. Their eyes lock.

"Me too," he murmurs.

This is too close. "Murphy, don't..."

"What? Don't connect to an actual human being instead of a computer? Instead of a weapon?" He leans in to kiss her.

She pulls back. "I've trusted people before. Every time I let myself... I've lost so much."

"I know. Me too. And yet the way you curve your mouth like that makes me all kinds of crazy..."

She smiles, and he kisses her. After a beat, she responds, leaning into him. This is okay. This feels right.

An alarm, blaring and urgent. They pull away and go to the windows. Outside, two land rovers driven by the teen boys speed up the drive and squeal to a stop. The boys jump out.

Maze and Murphy rush into the living area to see Thrash, Rainy, and the boys shoving guns and boxes of weapons inside secret wall compartments.

Murphy asks, "What's going on?"

"Nation vans headed this way," Thrash says. "You better take off."

"What about you?"

"They already know about us. We'll be all right."

"Nation knows you deal weapons?"

"Hell, man, they buy from us. They buy by the truckload. But they also steal from us, and it makes me cranky."

Maze grabs some guns, stuffs them in Murphy's bag.

Thrash holds up a handful of small, flat grenades. "These babies are my fave. Stick to anyfing—metal, rock, synth. They pack quite the punch. Gotta place them though, see? Stick them on."

Maze stuffs her pockets with them.

"This isn't a scheduled stop," Rainy says. "My guess is they're here because of you."

Maze stops, looks at Murphy. "I thought we were scrambled. How did they find us?"

"How should I know?"

Maze pulls Murphy's scrambling device from her pocket, drops it on the floor, and smashes it under her boot.

"Hey! That— Oh, man—"

"They found us anyway," she says. "It doesn't work." To Thrash and Rainy: "What's the best direction to go?"

"West. Try to lose them in the hills."

"You can just squeak by, I think," Thrash says.

Outside, Murphy and Maze jump in the truck. Rainy pushes a bag of food and water through the window. "Be careful out there," she says.

"Will you all be okay?" Maze asks.

Rainy nods. Murphy takes the truck down the drive and floors it, heading west.

The Null again. Nothing but sand. The sun is starting to sink, almost touching the low, rocky hills a distance away. The racing truck bounces along an old highway. Maze, laser pistol in hand, hangs on as she peers out the back window.

"Anything?" Murphy asks.

"I'm sure they won't notice the dust trail you're kicking up."

Murphy is defensive. "It's a desert. There's dust. Hey, I don't know how they tracked us, okay? But it wasn't—"

Then an ear-blasting throbbing sound. The truck rocks. They look at each other, then out the back window.

Four motorcycles driven by uniformed Nation cops roar up behind them. The bikes are black, with bulletproof bubble tops and big tires for going over sand.

Maze grips the dashboard as the truck lurches sideways, bounces. Murphy spins the wheel and it rights itself.

"What's that noise?"

"Sound waves! They want to push the truck over or blast our eardrums or both!" Murphy's voice cuts in and out amid the throbbing woob-woob.

Maze leans out the window and gets off rounds with the laser pistol. They bounce off the bubble tops. The thrum and throb is maddening. Murphy fights the wheel as the truck rocks and tips. Maze pulls herself back in, reloads. One motorcycle speeds up even with the truck. Maze tosses a grenade—it bounces harmlessly against the bubble top, then to the ground—

The next motorcycle goes over it just as it explodes—

Debris and the cop fly into the air. The other motorcycles move back a safe distance, the riders wary of more grenades.

Murphy nods. "One down!"

"Thrash said these should be stuck on!"

"What?"

He can't hear her. A barrage of thrums hits the back windshield. Maze and Murphy duck as glass shatters.

"I'm gonna try something!" he says. "It might be dangerous!"

Maze widens her eyes in mock alarm. "Oh no!"

Murphy gives a wry grin and spins the wheel. The truck veers off the road. Ahead of them is a vast, flat expanse of sand. "The first time I came to the Null," he shouts, "Thrash warned me to stay on the roads because of the sinkholes!"

His voice cuts in and out, but Maze gets the gist. "Won't we sink too?" she asks.

"Very possibly!"

Ahead are irregular circles of sand, big as swimming pools, that look a little different, wetter—but only if you know what to look for.

The motorcycles stay back, letting the sound waves do

their job. Murphy speeds up, navigating between sinkholes. The tires slog and slide. Murphy wrestles the steering wheel. Two motorcycles follow at an angle. Maze tosses more grenades to distract the riders. They dodge and weave to avoid the exploding grenades. The motorcycles suddenly fishtail as sand grabs at their tires. The riders fight to control their bikes—

One gets caught—

Then another—

The third rider realizes what's happening, steers a wide path. The others slog, sinking deeper, deeper.

The two motorcycles' tires are completely stuck. Stopped. Sinking. One rider falls off, thrashing in the sand. Both bikes sink fast. The riders follow, flailing.

Murphy grapples with the pulling sand, whips the truck, side tires upending, steers it away from the sinkhole field, and speeds away.

"You're more of a badass than I thought!" she tells him.

He grins.

The remaining cycle speeds up behind them, thrums blasting impossibly loud.

Maze points out the window. "Head for the rocks!"

The truck skids through the sand toward the low, rocky hills, the motorcycle on its heels.

Maze puts down her gun. She has one grenade left. She leans close to Murphy. "When we get to the rocks, can you angle the truck so I can slip out without them seeing?"

Murphy nods; no more time for talk, as the truck jounces along the uneven ground.

A giant boulder, bigger than the truck, cuts loose from the rocky slope and plummets across the truck's path. Smaller boulders follow, rolling and crashing around them. The motorcycle behind them easily veers between moving boulders.

Murphy swerves, tires screeching— "The sound waves are loosening them!"

The rocky hills then swallow the truck from view. Murphy barely slows down, and Maze opens her door just enough to slip out and tumble to the ground. She quickly scrambles behind boulders as Murphy drives on.

The motorcycle speeds up, weaves between boulders. The woob-woob is deafening—

Maze, grenade in her teeth, jumps up from her hiding place—

Leaps onto the back end of the bike—

The rider sees her—

Whips the bike back and forth to dislodge her—

Murphy's truck is blasted by a sound wave—

It glances off a tumbling rock—-

Careens over—

And explodes—

Maze sees this, almost spills off the bike but hangs on—

She sticks the grenade—

Lets go—

To land hard on the rocks.

The motorcycle explodes, flies slantways, and crashes into the hill.

The throb is gone.

Maze jumps to shaky feet—

"Murphy! MURPHY!"

She leaps from the rocks and races to the burning truck—

Makes it as Murphy struggles to get out—

She yanks his arms—

Murphy holds his bleeding leg as they both stagger to a safe distance.

Near the rocks, Maze and Murphy watch hopelessly as the truck burns. Weapons inside explode and shower them with sparks. Murphy ducks. Maze stares, rigid, at the fire.

Her weapons are gone. She's lost again.

"It'll be dark soon," Murphy says gently. "We have to find someplace to hole up."

She wipes blood from her mouth and turns away.

By evening, Murphy leans against Maze as they trudge across the sand. He licks dry lips and squints into the setting sun. The area is scattered with the remains of mobile homes—rusted aluminum walls, rotted furniture, broken glass.

Murphy stumbles, and Maze helps him slide to the ground near a crumbled bathtub. She checks his injured leg, then rips the sleeves off her shirt for bandages.

"Just a few minutes..." he gasps.

"We're both trashed," she says. "We're here for the night."

"It's too open—"

"We'll make a shelter. If it's as dangerous as you say, we can't just wander around in the dark."

He gives up, winces as she wraps the shirtsleeves around his leg and ties them.

"In the morning they'll send more cops," he says.

"Good. I've always wanted a motorcycle." She goes to a rusted aluminum panel and starts dragging it over.

Night. Maze and Murphy sit under a shelter of aluminum debris as the stars blanket them all around. Maze sharpens a piece of metal with a rock. A neat pile of more rocks, glass, and hard trash is next to her. Crickets chirp loudly.

"We can hunt for food when it gets light," she says.

Murphy, hefting a rock to test its weight, nods wearily. Maze doesn't see his nod and reaches a hand to his forehead.

"You okay?" she asks gently.

Their eyes lock.

"I bet you made an amazing nurse," he says.

Maze smiles softly and goes back to sharpening. "Sometimes before I fall asleep, I pretend the world is different. Like an alternate universe, you know? And in the morning I know I'll take Frankie to school, and then I'll go off to work at the hospital."

He chuckles. "This is your fantasy? Work and school? In mine, I'm hitting the high score in *Donkey Kong*. Then four hot cheerleaders carry me on their shoulders to my billion-dollar beach house where we drink tequila and play video games all night." He thinks a beat. "Okay, I'm still revising that last part."

They look out at the blanket of stars.

"Do you really have hope the world will get better?" she asks.

"Hmm?"

"You said that earlier."

"I...I do have hope," he says wearily. "It will take a lot of work. A lot of sacrifice."

"What more can people sacrifice when they've got nothing left?"

"I don't know." He touches her face.

The death scream of a distant animal makes them sit up, alert. The crickets are silent, then resume.

"You've been to the Null before," she says. "What was it?"

"Something that just got eaten by something else."

"We don't need to worry. It's too far away."

"Not for long."

She holds up the makeshift knife in the moonlight, tests it with her finger.

Murphy watches her. "Can I ask you something? These

people who make you kill for them... Have you ever tried to run away? Or find them and stop them?"

Maze shrugs. "When it started, I was alone. I didn't care. What's a life worth in this world? What's my life worth? I was hoping I'd make a mistake and they'd have an excuse to kill me." A beat. "Then I had my son, and it became a living. A job, which is more than most people have. It was money. I was saving up, and Frankie and I were gonna get out and go somewhere clean, where the air is fresh and you can see the sky. Somewhere like the desert."

The sudden animal shriek is close, loud. It sounds like a chicken being strangled with a chainsaw. Maze jumps up, knife ready.

Murphy grabs some rocks. "Yeah, it's a regular paradise out here."

Another animal shriek, and Maze whirls to the left—

"Ahhgh! My—leg!"

Maze spins to her right, sees something big yank Murphy to the ground—

"Murphy!" She rushes forward—

It's a Gila monster, massive, bigger than Murphy. Murphy pounds at it with a rock. It won't let go of his leg. "Ahhgh!!"

Maze jumps on it, rams her makeshift knife in its throat—

Blood flies as it roars and thrashes—

Murphy scrambles away—

Another giant lizard runs in from the dark—
Maze leaps, slashes with the knife—
It dodges, goes for her throat—
Then hisses and retreats under a hail of rocks thrown by Murphy—
A third one lumbers out fast from behind the shelter—
"Look out!"
Maze whirls just as it leaps at her—
They both tumble—
Her knife goes flying—
Maze and the lizard grapple—
But it's heavier, bigger, and it pins Maze to the sand—
Its jaws gape inches from her face—
Saliva drips—
The sudden glare of lights on the two—
Laser bullets rip through the monster's body—
And it collapses on top of her.

Maze, still pinned by the monster, wipes drool from her face—

Turns her head to see—

Two cops in black uniforms, laser guns aimed at her head. "Don't move!" a cop screams, very aggro. "Don't move, criminal!"

Maze sighs. "No problem."

Two more cops have their guns trained on Murphy as he gets to his feet, gasping, holding his mangled, bloody leg. Captain Jayks approaches, kicks at the lizard on top of

Maze to make sure it's dead.

Jayks nods at her. "Nice to finally meet you."

Minutes later, Maze, near an armored van, wipes lizard saliva from her face and arms. Jayks has a laser gun trained on her. Murphy sits nearby as a medic attends to his leg.

"That saliva is toxic," Jayks says. "Make sure it's all off or you'll be a sweating, hallucinating mess by morning."

Maze asks, "Do you know where my son is? Frankie?"

"I'm sorry, I don't. You know, our medic can take a look at your bullet wound."

She's surprised Jayks is so considerate. "I'm okay."

The aggro cop swaggers up. "Sir, perimeter is secure. All creatures have been deceased. If you like, I can emplace a charge field in case the criminal attempts escape. She'd be fried crisp in seconds."

"Er, that's okay, officer," Jayks replies. "We're heading out now."

The cop nods at Murphy. "What about our operative, sir?"

Maze, startled, looks at Murphy. Murphy freezes. His crushed expression reveals his guilt.

Jayks waves away his idiotic officer. "Guess he's riding with you now!"

Maze stalks up to Murphy. A beat. She's devastated. He can't meet her eyes.

"You work for Nation?" she asks.

He nods.

"You helped them catch me?"

He nods again. He can't speak.

She stares at him. There's nothing more to say. She shivers, suddenly so cold she knows she's finally dead inside. She brushes past him and climbs into the van.

III.

The room is sterile, white walls and ceiling, too brightly lit. Everything is made from molded synth-plastic material. Maze, wearing a paper-thin smock, slouches in a chair across from an empty desk.

Jayks sits off to the side. "Murphy seems like a good agent. But he likes to mess with people." He chuckles. "You two have that in common."

Maze says nothing, her expression blank.

The door opens, and in walks Rekk, seemingly pleasant, businesslike, a half-smile on his serene, middle-aged face. He wears a white lab coat. There's a small but noticeable red stain on the front. "Good evening," he says.

Maze watches Rekk with narrowed eyes. Rekk pulls an atomizer from his pocket, spray-disinfects the desk and chair, then sets the atomizer on the desk. He sits at the desk and pulls out a touchpad device the size of an iPhone.

"Let's begin," he says to Maze. Then, mildly: "Who do you work for?"

She's not going to put up with this crap. "Where's my son?"

A beat. Rekk tries again. "Who do you work for?"

"Where's my son?"

Jayks explains, "She thinks Nation kidnapped her little boy."

"Ah, I see." Rekk runs his fingers lightly on the touchpad. Maze tenses in pain as blue electrochemical pulses emanate from the chair, driving into her.

Rekk touches the pad again, and the blue pulses stop. Maze shudders, glares. She tries to go for Rekk, but a force field keeps her pinned in the chair. Again, Rekk touches the pad. Maze grimaces, draws tight, teeth clenched, fingers spasming on the arms of the chair. He stops it, and Maze sags, gasping.

"I... All ri—"

Rekk hits the button again. The pain gets worse each time. Maze screams.

"Okay, Christ, let her answer the question!" Jayks yells.

Rekk hits stop. Maze crumples in the chair. She's dazed. She's drugged from the chemicals.

Rekk, mildly: "Who do you work for?"

She'll cooperate. Anything to make it stop. "I get calls...with instructions. I don't know who it is."

Rekk's fingers hover over the touchpad—

Oh God. "I don't! I don't know who it is. I just do what they tell me. I get paid. And they leave my son and me alone."

"They instructed you to assassinate Misters Kellar and

Downey?"

She nods wearily. Rekk touches the touchpad. Maze screams again, tight and rigid against the chair.

Jayks stands. "Stop! Come on, what the hell? She's giving you what you want!"

Rekk hits stop. Maze slumps, half-conscious. If the chair's force field wasn't holding her, she'd drop to the floor.

Pleasant expression still on his face, Rekk turns to Jayks. "Captain Jayks, we are dealing with a dangerous political criminal with no morals or ethics. No doubt you follow a certain protocol with the degenerate herd in your zone. As you can see, I also follow a protocol."

"What I see is you using a little more 'protocol' than you need to, pal. And enjoying it."

"You may leave if you like."

Jayks frowns. "My protocol says I stay with the prisoner during the interrogation so you don't kill her."

Rekk dismisses him with a shrug and turns back to Maze. She struggles to keep her eyes open.

"Do you know of a group called Tropo?" She shakes her head. He looks at Jayks. "Do *you*?"

"Hum one of their tunes. Maybe I heard 'em on the radio."

"Humorous. Tropo is a cell of underground radicals. Anarchists. Political fundamentalists. They've participated in many crimes against Nation, including murder, and this detainee is an operative of theirs."

Maze licks at the corner of her dry mouth. "I don't give a crap about your politics...and I don't belong to any group...except the human race."

"And by the looks of you, barely that." Something beeps on Rekk's touchpad. His brow furrows as he reads it. "It appears I'm called away for now. We will discuss Tropo in our next session. Please be prepared to be more cooperative."

Maze painfully pulls herself to sit upright, gaze steady. "Go ahead. Press the button more. At least I still feel. You don't have a soul anymore. You're synthetic...a robot."

Rekk smiles. "And yet you yourself blindly followed instructions and performed tasks without question. For years." To Jayks: "Captain Jayks, will you please take the criminal to her cell?"

"Why can't you do it?"

"Oh, no. I don't actually touch them. They may carry...something."

Rekk releases the chair's force field. Jayks takes Maze's arm and helps her to her feet. He snaps a metal force band on her wrist.

She's unsteady, but she sneers at Rekk. "Got a little something on your coat there. Might be all kinds of fatal."

Rekk looks down to see the bloodstain. His hand waves over it like it's a bee. He's afraid to touch it. "Oh dear. Oh no. Assistance! Assistance!"

Maze looks satisfied as Jayks leads her out the door. Jayks tries to hide a grin himself. A burly, lab-coated assistant rushes past them into the room.

The corridors are just as bright white, just as sterile. Occasional uniformed Nation Headquarters employees busily stride by punching touchpads or talking into headsets. Jayks lets go of Maze's arm as he walks her along. She gains a little strength with each step.

Trilla appears at the end of the corridor with a dog on a makeshift leash.

Maze recognizes him. "Rowdy!"

Rowdy pulls on the leash, tries to get to Maze. Trilla holds on. "Hey, heel! Whoa!"

"Where's Harry? Harry!" Maze looks around wildly, tries to run toward the dog, but the metal force band keeps her close to Jayks.

Rowdy breaks free of the leash and bounds to Maze. She falls to her knees, hugs him tight. He licks her face.

"Hey, Rowds. Hey, boy." To Jayks, pissed: "Where is Harry? I want to see him. Now."

Trilla has joined them. "Criminal, you don't dictate orders. Stand up."

"It's okay, Trilla."

"Captain, I didn't know what to... Disposal will only unload deceased things, they said. A butcher will pay top dollar, though, because it's not that old and tough—"

Maze is up, in Trilla's face. "You hurt this dog and I

will claw out your intestines and feed them to you."

Trilla, alarmed, backs up, grabs her laser gun.

Jayks comes between them. "Easy, Trilla. Prisoner, back off!"

Maze won't back off, but her ferocity is quickly deflating to grief. "Please... Where's Harry?"

Another white interrogation room, but the lights are dimmed to a pinkish glow. Harry is in one of the molded synth chairs, his motorized chair in the corner. He's slumped and obviously dead. There's blood on his mouth where he bit his tongue.

Maze stands over his body, hand on his arm. This man saved her, kept her alive, and now she's caused his death. She whispers, "Harry... Harry..." She whispers, "Don't worry; I'll take care of Rowdy." She whispers, "Be well on your new journey."

She kisses his cheek. Then she takes a deep breath. She is beyond cold, beyond dead; she is stone. She walks up to Jayks and Trilla, who holds Rowdy by his leash.

Jayks doesn't know what to say. She's his prisoner—but she's a person too. "I... He never said a word."

Trilla looks at Jayks, who nods. Trilla gives Maze the leash.

Maze's cell is a tall, skinny tube of clear plastic. Everything is clear, including the bed and toilet. A hundred tubes are crammed together—prisoners so close, but separated by clear synth walls. Dozens of prisoners in tubes around Maze sleep or slouch with their heads down.

She ignores them, curls up on the floor with her arms around Rowdy. She closes her eyes.

—

Murphy, weary, unkempt, bandage under his shredded, bloody pant leg, limps into his apartment.

Vozer rises impatiently from the couch. We recognize him as the scruffy, scarred man from the diner. His voice is the voice on Maze's phone. "Gee, Murph. Take a detour to granny's house?"

Murphy doesn't hesitate. He lurches to Vozer, hauls off and punches him in the face. Vozer stumbles back and hits the couch.

Murphy is enraged. "You told me you hired her! You told me she was doing these jobs of her own free will and you were paying her!"

"What the hell? I am paying her—!"

"You were threatening her and her little boy! Where is he? You told me she had nothing, no one, that she had a death wish, that she was crazy!"

Vozer makes it to his feet, holding his jaw. "And that's why we keep you away from day-to-day operations, Murph. You're better with machines than people. I said get her captured fast, not after you went on a honeymoon in the desert."

"If it looked too easy, she would have caught on."

"Big whatever. Did you take care of the bug or not?"

"It's taken care of."

Lina, a wiry and tired-looking thirty-year-old, approaches holding a sleepy, fussing Frankie in her arms. "Thanks for nothing, guys. It took me a long time to get him to sleep. And now he's not."

Murphy notices them for the first time, as well as two Tropo men sleeping on chairs—the men who kidnapped Frankie.

Frankie reaches for Murphy's hand. Murphy takes it. "Hey, Frankie. Hi, guy. Are you a sleepy guy?"

He turns to Vozer, keeping an even tone so Frankie doesn't get upset. "You scum. You killed an innocent old woman and kidnapped a child. Do you know what hell his mother's going through?"

Frankie squirms and fusses. Lina gives up, dumping him in Murphy's arms.

Vozer rubs his scarred face. "She had a job to do! This isn't daycare. We're all making sacrifices. How many thousands of people are suffering, starving, dying because of Nation and its false promises, its greed?" Vozer shrugs. "One old woman. One crazy chick."

"You're singing the same tired song, Vozer," Murphy says. "I used to sing it too."

"Oh, and now you've got a frog in your throat?"

Murphy shakes his head. "Do you even have a plan? What happens now? We gather Tropo's meager dozens and just waltz in?"

"Yeah! Exactly. We get in and take over. Because they won't be able to stop us. Information, my friend. Information is power. We don't need an army." Vozer pulls out his laser gun. "Now cut the crap and let's see what she's up to."

Murphy notes the threatening edge to Vozer's voice, his too-bright eyes. He goes to his computers, protectively sits Frankie on his lap, and types on a keyboard. Data scrolls across the screen.

Vozer keeps the gun in his hand. "Is it transmitting?"

Murphy, reluctantly: "It's transmitting."

"Floor plans, weapons, guards?"

"Yes."

"Satellite?"

"It'll take a while for all the data to get through, but yes."

Lina peers over their shoulders. "Why can't we just get a visual of Nation HQ like for other places?"

Murphy says, "Their firewall is too strong. We needed a bug inside."

"It only works if the host is alive. It gets its power from their skin temperature. They go out, it goes out." Vozer beams, pleased with himself. "We needed the best, and she's the best. She might even make it out of there alive."

Murphy says, "If she does, you better hope she doesn't find you."

—

Maze dozes on the floor of her cell. The lights are dimmed to a pinkish glow. Rowdy sniffs at the gluestitched wound on Maze's stomach, whines. Puts a paw on it.

Maze jolts awake. "Rowdy...you okay? What is it?"

The dog seems obsessed with the wound—or something inside it. He whines again, pushes his nose in Maze's stomach.

"Rowds, hey, hey." She's intrigued by his behavior. She feels the gluestitch with her fingers. She pauses, then begins to peel it off.

A little blood seeps—

Grimacing, she digs at the wound with her fingers—

And pulls out a tiny electronic button.

A bug.

Her expression goes deadly. "Murphy."

She tosses the bug into the toilet. Pulses of air and light puff out—

The bug disintegrates.

Maze notices someone watching from a cell next door—Crux, the feral teen from the park. He's got bruises and cuts on his face and arms.

"Haven't seen a dog in, like, ten years," Crux says. "I hear they taste like synth-meat."

Maze ignores him, resealing her wound.

Crux gives a fierce grin, showing his filed, pointy teeth. "Wait. I know you. You led Nation cop goons into the park and they shot my girlfriend."

Murphy, sitting in front of his computer, stares uncomprehendingly. The screen now shows a cursor and the words 'No Data.'

Frankie sleeps in his lap. Vozer nods off in a nearby chair.

"Um...shouldn't that be showing something?" Lina leans over Murphy's shoulder. Murphy can't move—he's in shock. He's in anguish.

Lina says again, "I thought you said she had to be alive for it to... Oh."

Vozer rouses. From behind them he peers at the screen. "No way..." He freaks out, stomping around the room. "We need her! We need that data! How much did we get?"

Murphy sags in his chair. "I don't know."

Frankie squirms, wakes up, and starts crying. The two Tropo men wake up, yawning.

"Looks like...twenty percent?" Lina says.

"What can we do with twenty percent?"

"Get our asses shot off," Lina says.

Vozer waves his laser pistol in her face. "You're not helping!"

She flips him the bird.

Vozer stomps around some more. "Maybe there's a glitch in the satellite. It could be a million things, right? We can find out, right?" To Murphy: "Okay, genius. They think you work for Nation, so locate one of your Nation buddies and find out what went wrong."

Murphy hugs Frankie to comfort him. It's all he can manage. "Get out, Vozer," he rasps. "I'm done."

Vozer considers. Points his pistol. "Give me the kid and I'll go."

"I'm keeping him. And if his mother is alive after all, I'll make sure she's reunited—"

Vozer shoots. Murphy recoils, scorched blood bursting from his shoulder inches from Frankie's head. Frankie lets out a loud wail.

"Vozer—!"

Vozer waves his pistol at Frankie. "Give up the brat, or the next shot goes through him to you."

Murphy tries to shield Frankie with his body, but the little boy writhes and cries. Vozer shrugs and takes aim. Lina turns away.

"Okay!" Murphy cries. "Okay. Okay."

Vozer smiles in satisfaction. He nods at Lina, who takes Frankie from Murphy's arms and carries him out the door. The two Tropo men follow her.

"You get him back when you find out what's going on at HQ." Vozer smirks. "Call me." He leaves.

Murphy crumples in his chair, head in his arms.

—

Maze tries to sleep, but Crux leans full length against the clear wall inches away, staring at her. She opens her eyes.

"They were showing your story on Celebrity Realnews,"

Crux says. "I liked the part where you blew up the Catatrons. Man, you're gonna go out in a blaze of glory, aren't you? Wish I could do that."

Maze gives a wry smile. "Why did they capture you?"

"Target practice on some drones. But they shoot back now. Next thing I know, I wake up here." He shakes his head. "You're gonna go out in a blaze of glory. Me? I'm gonna end up like melted mush in a torture chair. Death sucks."

Two guards in black, armed and blank-faced, come to Maze's cell. One opens the electronic door and motions to Maze. Rowdy growls.

"Hey, can you keep an eye on my dog?" she asks Crux.

Crux shrugs. "Okay."

She gives Rowdy a big hug, pets him vigorously. The dog relaxes. "I guess just talk to him. He likes that."

"No sweat." Crux eyes the dog.

"And don't try to eat him."

Crux grins.

The guards enter Maze's cell. One snaps a metal force band on her wrist. Now she's helpless.

In the white room, Rekk sits at his desk with his hands folded around his touchpad. He's changed into a nonstained white lab coat. His atomizer is on the desk. Anders Woo, presidential candidate, paces the room. His slick gameshow-host smile is pasted to his face.

Maze covers her shock at seeing Woo. The guards sit

Maze in the torture chair, remove the wristband, and leave.

On a giant wall TV screen, masses of people fill the square, cheering, chanting. Anders Woo waves to the crowd from a podium. A caption on the screen reads: 'Woo Elected President.' Then a montage, quick scenes of more masses of people in front of video screens in other zones. All cheering. All happy.

Maze stares at the TV in disgust. "That's a lie. You faked the crowds. You faked the election."

Rekk says pleasantly, "Hello again, criminal."

"That's a big lie," Maze says again, glaring.

Woo brushes at the air as if at a fly. "Now, I've asked Mister Rekk here to forego using his...uh, usual means of persuasion for a few minutes so we can just talk informally. Does that sound all right?"

Maze narrows her eyes.

"I've been informed that you're a member of an underground cell called Tropo. Is that right?"

Maze doesn't answer.

"Tropo has been behind a number of terrorist acts for the past few years, including assassinations. For most of these I assume you were the perpetrator."

"Eight in the past three years, Leader—er, President Woo."

Woo acts impressed. "Eight killings in the past three years. My. And I guess I was the next target?"

Maze sneezes noisily, leans her face down to her sleeve

and wipes her nose. "Sorry. Little cold. My cell was drafty."

Rekk recoils, picks up the atomizer, and sprays around himself—a mist barrier. Maze takes note of his reaction.

Woo glances at Rekk, annoyed, then back to Maze. "Young lady, you may smirk, but Nation needs strong leadership. And thanks to you and your friends, I've filled that very urgent role. A real election at this point would have just wasted everyone's time. We start the Rebuild in the morning."

"You could have looked for candidates outside the wall."

Rekk gives a short laugh.

Woo smirks. "Yes, well... Have you ever heard of a particularly savage young man named Vozer? He sports a distinctive scar on his cheek. Mr. Vozer has been at the top of a short list of criminals we've been hunting for some time. I say short list because Nation doesn't stand for this sort of nonsense."

"Nation stands for nonsense of another sort?" Maze asks.

Woo's slick smile falters. "Do you work for Vozer? Is he connected with Tropo? Who else do you work with in your attempts to bring down Nation?"

"You seem to think I've done all these things. But I'm just a rat living on the other side of the wall."

"I know you've done these things, and you will answer my questions."

Maze cocks her head and says matter-of-factly, "Squeak. Squeak. Squeak."

Woo's smile is now a twisted monster in a clenched jaw. "Young lady, there will be a reckoning. I will lead Nation to a better place, believe me. Despite the efforts of you and your troupe of clowns, the Rebuild will happen as scheduled."

Woo nods at Rekk. Rekk taps his touchpad. Maze goes rigid in her chair as the blue pulses pump out. She bites her lip to stop a scream. Rekk taps again and she sags in the chair, gasping.

Rekk says mildly, "We would like the names and locations of your cohorts."

"I don't know any names— Oh God—"

Rekk taps the touchpad, and this time Maze screams, spasming.

—

Jayks, the beginnings of a scruffy beard on his face, sits in his office watching Woo make his acceptance speech in holographic 3-D.

With a satisfied smile, Woo waits until the cheers stop. "Thank you. Thank you, people of Nation, for voting for me. Please watch tomorrow morning when I present my State of Nation speech. We've had crews out repairing all the public screens, so be sure to gather 'round them wherever you may be. Don't disappoint me."

A knock on the door, and Murphy pokes his head in.

He watches Woo's image. He frowns.

"Murphy. Come in. How's the leg?"

Murphy shrugs, hobbling in. "Only hurts when I'm alive. I...just wanted to follow up on the prisoner, what information you've gotten."

"Oh. Well, I can't discuss an ongoing investigation."

Murphy, hopeful: "So it's still ongoing? I mean, the prisoner is...still ongoing?"

Jayks gives him a thoughtful look.

—

Maze slumps in the chair, eyes fluttering. She wants to sleep. She knows it's dangerous to let herself sleep, but she wants it so badly.

Woo leans close and peers at her. "Mr. Rekk, typically how long can a criminal withstand your chair?"

"My, no one's ever asked me that before. A gentleman I worked with just recently took quite a few hours to...break."

That wakes her up. "He didn't break..."

"I'm sorry, what was that?"

"Harry didn't break." She painfully lifts her head. Her eyes go dangerous.

Woo's slick smile comes back broader than ever. "But you will, young lady." To Rekk: "Let's move this a little faster. "

Rekk nods. His fingers tap the touchpad. Maze shrieks, body convulsing. It goes on and on. When Rekk hits stop,

Maze is limp, liquid. She thinks she might really be dead. Blood drips from her mouth where she bit her tongue.

She's surprised when she can open her eyes. "Okay."

"Yes, criminal?"

"Okay... Please. I'll tell you. I can make them come out of hiding. We...send our retinal scans online—"

"Those can be altered—"

"They're encrypted. I send my retinal scan. The database verifies it...and then whoever I send my scan to sends their scan. It's a signal. I can find whoever you want."

Woo looks dubious. Rekk's finger poises over the touchpad.

Oh God. "Wait. Please. I don't know how else to do it."

Woo's brow furrows as he considers. Then: "All right. We'll give this a try. Mr. Rekk, let her use your touchpad."

"Why?"

"So she can scan her damn eyeball and send it. Give her—"

"I'm sorry. I can't do that." Rekk's voice breaks. He holds his touchpad up and away like a child.

"Rekk, give her your touchpad. That's an order from Nation."

Rekk is physically torn between doing his duty and keeping the germs away.

Woo pulls a laser gun from a holster under his coat. "I'll keep this pointed at her. All right?"

Rekk swallows painfully. "I'll...scan it."

"Well, just do something!"

"Yes, sir."

Rekk edges toward Maze. He holds out the touchpad, screen facing Maze, keeping his body as far away as he can. She tries to lean forward but the chair confines her.

Woo sighs. "Closer, Mr. Rekk."

Rekk pushes the touchpad closer to Maze's face.

Maze shakes with effort. "No, I have to steady it."

Rekk looks to Woo, who nods, aiming the gun. Rekk taps the screen, and one of Maze's hands is free. Maze tries to reach the touchpad, but she can't. Her hand is weak. Rekk reluctantly moves closer, squeezing his eyes shut.

"Dog hair?"

Rekk's eyes pop open.

Maze clumsily brushes at her smock. Rowdy's hair flies. "I've got filthy dog hair all over me!"

Rekk shrieks—

Maze's hand flashes out, wrenches the touchpad from Rekk's grasp. She quickly touches the screen in combinations. She's free of the chair.

Rekk stumbles back and smacks the edge of the desk. Maze grabs the taser from his belt. Woo shoots at Maze but she dives—

Tackles him—

Wrestles him for the gun—

She pushes the taser into his side—

Woo crumples as he's tazed.

She grabs the gun. She goes for Rekk.

"Assista—!" Maze tazes Rekk and he drops, whimpering. She drags him toward the torture chair.

"No! No!"

Maze slams Rekk's head onto the chair seat. He pushes at her desperately, and she tazes him again.

"This is for Harry." She touches the touchpad. Rekk's head is held by the force field—

She turns on the blue juice—

Rekk's eyes roll back in his head. His scream becomes a high-pitched whine—

She grabs Woo. "Come on...Mister President."

Leaving Rekk to fry, she drags Woo to his feet.

IV.

In the bright corridor, Maze keeps the gun snug against Woo's side. Still affected by the taser, Woo wanders where Maze directs him. She shuffles along beside him like she's his prisoner. It's quiet, late. What few Nation employees there are give a polite nod and walk past.

Outside the synth tube cells, Maze fiddles with the touchpad.

Crux looks surprised to see her. "He whined a little but he was fine."

Maze's cell door swings open. Rowdy trots out.

"Can I come with you?" Crux asks.

Maze nods and presses the touchpad screen. Crux's

door swings open. She presses the screen again. More cell doors swing open. Two dozen prisoners look up sleepily.

"There's something sticking out of his collar." Crux points.

Maze stoops to Rowdy's collar and pulls out a toothpick-sized device. She inspects it.

"What is it?"

"A gift from a friend?" She notices it will fit into a port in the touchpad. She inserts it.

Crux and Woo regard each other with pure hatred. Crux spits on the floor.

—

A knock on Jayks's office door, and Trilla enters. "Captain, sorry—the criminal has escaped."

Murphy covers up a giant grin of relief. Jayks sighs and grabs a weapon. Murphy grabs a weapon too.

Jayks says, "Trilla, I'd prefer you call them prisoners, not criminals."

"I'm only going by Nation rules, Captain."

"I know, but 'criminal' implies they're already guilty."

She's truly puzzled. "But aren't they?"

—

Crux drags Woo down the corridor. Rowdy tags behind. Maze keeps glancing at the touchpad screen.

"Anything?" Crux asks.

"It's just garble. We have to decode it somehow." Maze notices Woo seems very interested in the garble. "Do you know what this is?" she demands.

Woo just smiles his slick smile. Crux shows Woo the taser—Woo flinches and moves back. Maze leads them to an elevator and they all get in.

Maze takes a deep breath. "See the ball. Be the ball."

"Huh?" Crux asks.

"I heard it in a movie once. I think it means if you can see it, like in your mind? Then you can do it."

Crux is in awe. "Will you be my girlfriend?"

The door closes. Innocuous Muzak plays.

Woo seems to be recovering. "Leave me here," he says. "I won't call the guards."

"Tropo wants you dead," Maze says. "But I'm keeping you very alive. You're my ticket to my son."

"Why should I help you if I know you won't kill me?" Woo asks.

Crux slugs him. Woo doubles over. "There are worse things than being dead, sucker."

The door opens to the lobby—

A dozen Nation guards aim laser rifles at them. When they see Woo, they hesitate. Maze and Crux duck back, pulling Woo with them.

"Shoot, you fools!" Woo shouts.

A tense beat as they all look at each other. Then snipers on balconies above suddenly start firing. The shots divert around Woo toward Maze and Crux—

"Aw, hell, the bullets are programmed!" Crux yells.

Maze thrusts her gun into Woo's side. "Tell them to stand down!"

Woo just regards her with disgust and pity. Crux grins and goes to slug Woo again—

Then is hit with gunfire.

Crux blinks at the big, bleeding hole in his gut—

Looks at Maze—

Shrugs—

Leans over and gives her a sloppy, fervent kiss.

"Blaze of glory!" Crux yells. He barrels out the elevator screaming like a banshee. The guards, startled, shoot wildly. "Blaze of glory, scumsuckers! See the ball, be the ball!"

Crux grabs the nearest guard's throat—

And rips it out with his teeth. Blood flies. Crux slams the guard to the floor and takes his rifle—

Shoots at the other guards—

Crux, to Maze: "Run!"

Maze swivels, shoots, uses Woo as a shield—

She starts to run with Woo, Rowdy ahead—

Hesitates, glances back at Crux—

Maybe she can help him—

Crux whoops, spraying the guards with laser rounds—

The guards shoot back—

Crux is hit—

Again—

He drops to his knees, still shooting—

He's hit again—

His eyes droop...

Crux falls over.

Maze knows it's too late. She pulls Woo to the doors—

Laser bullets whiz past her—

Maze bursts out the doors to the square with Woo and Rowdy—

Twenty more guards stand in a line, guns pointed.

Maze and Rowdy duck—

As two dozen released prisoners, shouting and screaming, rush out the doors and scatter. The guards, panicked, shoot everywhere—

Some give chase—

Maze drags Woo toward the parking garage filled with solar cars and motorcycles. In the shadows, a car squeals up next to Maze.

It's Murphy. "Get in."

"Are you kidding me?" She's not getting in his car.

Woo suddenly struggles, pulls free—

She goes to grab him—

Murphy shoots—

Hits Woo in the shoulder. He drops.

"I need him alive!" Maze cries.

Shouts from across the square—Nation guards.

"Get in!" Murphy shouts again.

Maze relents, hauling Woo to his feet. She throws Woo in the back seat and then piles in after Rowdy. The car takes off.

The waterfront. The water is dark and thick and oily. There are no lights, no video screens. Murphy pulls up and parks. Maze is out of the car before it fully stops. Woo slumps in his seat, Rowdy guarding. Murphy gets out.

Maze, enraged: "You used me. You screwed with me. You put a bug in me??"

"We needed you inside. I had to plant the bug and let you get caught so you could transmit back to us. We've tried to get inside before. No one has ever survived, let alone gotten back out."

"Wait, what?"

"I was really working for Tropo."

"A spy against Nation." She shakes her head. "And you couldn't give me a hint what you were doing?"

"You had your own agenda. You wouldn't have agreed to ours." He reaches to touch her.

She raises her gun. "You're right."

"I'm sorry. I wanted to tell you a million times."

"Why shouldn't I kill you?"

"I know who has Frankie."

She immediately lowers the gun. "Is he okay?"

A few minutes later, Murphy's holding his phone. "Ready?"

Maze nods. Murphy dials. Listens.

"Vozer. You were right. She is the best. And you're lucky she wants to make a deal." He hands the phone to Maze.

"Let me see Frankie," she says.

The phone's video screen splits. Vozer motions to Lina to bring Frankie. He points the phone near the toddler's face, and Frankie's and Maze's faces appear on each half of the screen.

"Frankie, sweetie? It's Mommy."

Frankie beams. "Mommy!"

"Punkin... How's my good boy?"

Vozer pulls the phone away, cuts the video. "There. Wasn't I a gracious host? Now it's your turn."

"I have Anders Woo."

"So kill him. Solve your third problem. Do your job."

"You kill him. Do whatever you want with him. Give me my son and you can have him. If not, I'll give him back to Nation with his greasy head still on."

Vozer grins. It's scary and maniacal. "Let's meet. Nation Square. Near the arch." He hangs up.

Maze and Murphy get back in the car. Murphy notices the touchpad, sees the garble still running across the screen. "May I?" He picks it up, starts tapping on the screen.

"Harry said it was something big, I know, but we don't have time—!"

Murphy, already done decoding, is dumbfounded by what he reads. "Where did you get this?"

"Harry must have hidden it in Rowdy's collar before he was captured, for me to find." Maze reads what's on the screen. She puts a hand to her mouth to stifle a moan.

"It's not a Rebuild," Murphy says. "It's genocide."

"How are they capable of killing so many people at once?" Then she realizes. "The video screens..."

"Ah, man, I built them the remotes! The screens must be programmed to do something during Woo's State of Nation tomorrow. Explode? Emit gas? But we have Woo."

"He already recorded the speech. He doesn't have to be live." Maze turns to consider Woo sprawled in the car, bleeding, half-conscious, Rowdy guarding him. An anguished beat. "I…I have to get my son."

Murphy nods, and they both check the clips in their laser pistols.

"Who do you work for now?" Maze asks. "Nation? Tropo?"

"I used to. Now I work for myself. I trade."

She takes a deep breath. "Will you help me with this trade?"

"I will."

A cold pre-dawn wind blows debris across the square. Maze and Murphy wait, wary and armed, under the crumbling arch. Footsteps. Maze turns. Vozer comes around the corner—

Maze is face-to-face with the voice on the phone, her puppet master, at the same time her ticket to a better life.

"Where's Frankie?" she asks, keeping her voice steady.

Vozer cocks his head, genuinely pleased. "We've only talked on the phone, but I feel like I know you. Isn't that funny?"

"The games are over, Vozer," Murphy says, weary.

"Ah, but they're not. There's something else I want. The layout, the guard stations, the satellite information from Nation Headquarters. I want that."

Maze is ready to explode. She grips her pistol with shaking hands. "I destroyed the bug. Give me my son and you get Woo."

Movement out of the corner of her eye in the semidark. Lina, holding a sleepy Frankie, comes toward them from a few yards away.

Vozer notices. "Lina! Dammit!"

"Frankie!" Maze makes a dash—

Vozer grabs his pistol, aims at her—

Murphy leaps, tackles him—

Vozer pistol whips him—

Sirens blast—

Lights glare—

Captain Jayks rushes forward, gun aimed. "Freeze! On the ground!"

Vozer shoots multiple rounds—

Jayks goes down—

Vozer takes off in the semidark.

Maze runs to Lina under the arch, pulls Frankie from her, hugs him tight and kisses him. The toddler grins. "Frankie, punkin. Oh God. How's my boy?"

"He's a cute kid." Lina gives a small smile. "Not all of

us in Tropo are like Vozer. We just wanted to help. We just wanted to make everyone free."

Maze considers Lina's words.

Laser shots ring past them. Maze ducks. Lina, in the line of fire, crumples to the stone. Maze takes off, holding Frankie. Two cops dash past a dying Lina after Maze.

"Freeze, criminal! Stop!"

Trilla and more cops appear in the square. Trilla rushes to Jayks. "Captain!"

Jayks weakly tries to sit up. Blood pours from his chest. "It was Vozer."

Murphy groggily gets to his feet. Trilla turns to see Murphy stumble off in the dark.

Jayks is losing consciousness fast. "Trilla..." he whispers, "you're in charge."

Maze and Frankie make it to the car parked in a dark alley. Rowdy, inside with Woo, starts barking—

A scraping of feet—

Vozer rushes her—

She twists, protecting Frankie—

Vozer points his laser gun and grabs hers. "Drive."

As the first hazy sunlight streaks red in the sky, Maze, behind the wheel, steers the car straight for the glassed front entrance of Nation Headquarters and floors it—

Guards scatter—

The car crashes through the glass and screeches to a stop.

Trilla kneels in the square next to Jayks and checks her touchpad, sees via camera Vozer, Maze, Frankie, and Woo get out of the car in the lobby of Nation Headquarters. Into her headset she orders, "Evacuate all remaining Nation HQ employees out the back. Now."

Inside the lobby it's deserted, dim. Vozer pushes Woo and Maze, who carries Frankie, toward the elevators. Rowdy trots along with them.

When an elevator door slides open, Vozer shoves the gun into Woo's side. "Satellite Control, please." Woo, holding his bleeding shoulder, reluctantly presses the button for floor ten.

"We haven't formally met," Vozer says. "I'm the head of Tropo. You know what 'Tropo' means? It means 'change.'"

Woo spits blood on the floor. "I thought it meant 'scum.'"

Tenth floor. Vozer ushers them into a huge room of computers and video screens: all of Nation's zones under the thumb of the main Nation HQ network. Maze hangs back, looking for escape, but Vozer pushes her forward again—

Rekk's touchpad drops from Maze's hand. Vozer lights up as he notes the Nation logo on it. "Did I just hear an angel sing? You didn't have this all along, did you?"

"It won't work for you, Vozer," Maze lies. "It's programmed to Nation employees."

"Like Leader Woo here?" Vozer picks it up and shows it to Woo. "You can communicate with the network with this, right? I want to bring Nation to its knees."

Maze backs up a step, clutching Frankie.

"I won't help you," Woo says.

Vozer frowns, touchpad still raised.

Maze kicks Vozer's hands—

The touchpad goes flying—

Woo punches Vozer—

The men grapple—

The touchpad clatters to the floor.

Maze grabs it—

And bolts out the door with Frankie, Rowdy running after.

Maze barrels down flight after flight of stairs with Frankie in her arms. She hits the fifth-floor landing and stops, gasping.

A low growl on the dark stairs below. Maze peers over the railing. "Rowdy?"

Rowdy next to her whines.

The clacking of metallic claws...

Then a snarl—clangy, electronic.

"Oh God." No.

The Giant Catatron growls savagely and bounds up the stairs straight for them. It's repaired. Shiny, new, and lethal.

Frankie screams. Maze yanks at the fire door—

It won't budge—

The Giant Catatron is almost upon them—

Rowdy jumps in front of Maze and Frankie, barking furiously—

The Giant Catatron stops up short—

And hisses—

As Rowdy barks savagely in its face—

Maze, to Frankie: "Hold on, punkin."

Frankie grabs tightly to her—

Maze jumps to the railing, slides down on her hip to the next floor—

Then the next railing to the next floor—

The Giant Catatron blinks at the barking Rowdy—

Then shakes its massive head, turns—

And clatters down the stairs after Maze—

She gets to the third-floor landing.

A door opens—

Murphy pulls Maze and Frankie through and slams the door, just as the Giant Catatron leaps—

And smashes against it.

Murphy grabs Maze and Frankie tight against him. "God, I was worried."

They can hear the Giant Catatron bang and crash against the door, its metallic snarls.

She says, "Last time it followed me by a tracking bullet. This time I think it's tracking my DNA."

The door buckles. One more crash, and the Giant Catatron is through—

Murphy and Maze, with Frankie, sprint down the corridor, the Giant Catatron on their heels. Murphy turns, shoots. Laser bullets bounce off its metallic hide. It doesn't even slow down.

—

A police perimeter has been set up in the square across from Nation Headquarters. Jayks, mostly alert now, sits near an ambulance as a medic finishes with bandages. The medic goes into the ambulance to clean up.

Trilla approaches, her usual reserve replaced by joy. "Captain!" She almost hugs him, but she stops, awkward. "Captain." She pats his arm.

Jayks, weary: "What've you got?"

She shows him her touchpad. On-screen, Murphy and Maze carrying Frankie run for their lives from the Giant Catatron.

Jayks looks grave. "Trilla, no."

"It will go after only her."

"But Murphy could get in the way—"

She gets defensive. "If he's protecting her, then he's guilty too."

"And the child?"

"Look, you put me in charge. Anyway, once the Cat is activated, it won't stop until it fulfills its assignment."

Jayks gives her a heavyhearted stare. "Oh, Trilla."

On the third floor of Nation HQ, Maze carries a screaming Frankie and follows Murphy through another door—

Slams it just as the Giant Catatron bashes against it—

"This won't hold."

Frankie struggles and jumps from Maze's arms to the floor—

Takes off at a trot—

"Frankie!"

The door crashes open and the Giant Catatron bursts in—

Its tracking eye zeros in on the toddler's movement—

Lunges toward him—

"Nooo!" Murphy jumps in the Giant Catatron's path—

It crashes into Murphy, sends him flying into an elevator door.

Maze grabs up her son, backing away from the raging, snarling Giant Catatron. There's nowhere to run—

Murphy gets to unsteady feet, shakes his head to clear it—

He blinks at the elevator—

His fingers find the Up button—

Maze catches on to what he's doing—

And she bolts at top speed for the elevator door—

The Giant Catatron in hot pursuit—

The elevator slides open—

Murphy presses the tenth-floor button—

Maze, clutching Frankie, inches from the open door, pivots at the last minute—

The Giant Catatron scrambles, tries to stop—

Slides into the elevator—

The door closes—

A crash from inside the elevator—

But it holds. The elevator rises.

"Let's go." Murphy heads for the stairs.

Maze doesn't move. "How do we make sure they don't blow up the screens?"

"There's no time. We need to get out—"

"Everyone outside the wall will be murdered," she says.

Murphy pauses.

"I'm not running anymore," she says.

Murphy sighs.

"How many remotes have to be destroyed?"

He shakes his head. "No, they all have to route through Satellite Control's network. Destroy that and you stop the bombs."

"Satellite Control is upstairs."

He realizes what she's saying. The Giant Catatron is up there now. "You don't have to do this," he says.

"Somebody has to try. Why not me?"

"Maybe Vozer destroyed it."

"You want to take the chance?"

"Then I'll do it."

She touches his arm. "You have to trust me. This is

what I do. Plus, Rowdy's still up there."

They lock eyes. He knows she's right. "Okay. Then let's really make some noise."

Murphy takes the touchpad, pulls off the back cover. His fingers move some of the guts around. He closes it back up. Hands it to Maze. She hands him Frankie.

"You be a good boy, punkin." She strokes Frankie's hair. Then to Murphy: "If I don't make it—"

He interrupts by pulling her into a long kiss. She kisses him back. They break and gaze at each other.

"You'll have two minutes after it's activated. It's all I could get you."

"What activates it?" she asks.

"Your voice."

He touches her lips. She nods silently. He taps the touchpad screen a last time. She presses the button to the other elevator. The door opens and she gets on.

Their eyes stay locked until the door closes.

Murphy holds Frankie tight and heads for the stairwell.

—

Outside Nation HQ, Trilla looks up from her touchpad to Jayks. "They're going to destroy Satellite and prevent the Rebuild."

She starts to call to the guards nearby—

Jayks grabs her, puts a hand over her mouth— "I'm sorry, Trilla."

His other arm encircles her neck. She fights him. He

hangs on. She chokes. Her touchpad clatters to the concrete.

"Things have to change," he says.

Trilla weakens. Her eyes slowly close. Jayks hangs on.

—

Tenth floor: the lights are dim. Maze pokes her head out the elevator door and carefully enters the corridor. She makes her way toward Satellite Control.

A noise from the stairwell—

She whirls—

Rowdy trots up to her. She smiles and hugs him.

In the Satellite Control room, Woo lies in a pool of blood. Maze moves fast past him to the mainframe.

"You have one more problem to handle tonight."

Maze turns. Vozer comes out of the shadows, face bruised and bloodied.

"Aren't you going to ask what it is?"

Maze says nothing, clutching the touchpad. Vozer notices. He points his laser pistol.

"That's what I was looking for. The mainframe is encoded. But I bet that unlocks it. Toss it over."

She just looks at him.

"You and I aren't all that different," he says. "I want a better world too."

She sighs. "Vozer, in less than one hour, everything outside the inner zone of Nation will be leveled by bombs planted in the video screens. Those who survive will be rounded up and murdered. That's what Woo meant by a

Rebuild. Is that a better world to you?"

Vozer barely blinks. He smiles. "I understand. Resources are low. And Nation has been excellent at keeping the riffraff out and the strong in. A balance, you might say. I underestimated Mister Woo. Think of the courage it takes to set something like this in motion."

"Why am I not surprised you'd say that."

Vozer shrugs and shoots—

Maze ducks as the bullet grazes her—

She barrels straight into Vozer and they both crash against computers and equipment.

Vozer pistol whips her, but she rolls, staggers up—

She kicks his hand, but he won't let go of the pistol—

Vozer grabs for the touchpad—

They wrestle for it—

Vozer elbows her hard in the stomach—

She cringes back—

He shoves the pistol at Maze's chest, his finger on the trigger…

There's movement behind Vozer—

Only Maze sees it—

The Giant Catatron slinks behind Vozer, tracking eye on Maze. It moves closer—

Maze says, gasping, "Know what, Vozer? I'd rather live in the filth with the rats. They're better people."

Vozer hears the low snarl, whirls just as the Giant Catatron leaps—

"Noooo—!"

It slams him against a panel of computers—

Where he crumples and is still.

Maze dodges, jumps out of the way—

Turns to face the electronic beast as it rushes her. "Come and get it, kitty!"

She tosses the touchpad at the Giant Catatron. It leaps, catches the touchpad, swallows it in one gulp—

And keeps coming.

"Dammit!"

Maze dodges again, but the Giant Catatron seizes her arm—

Its momentum crashes them both through a window—

Its head and front legs hang—

Maze dangles ten stories by her arm from the Giant Catatron's jaws—

Dusty morning sunlight reflects on the metal—

She writhes in pain—

Rowdy appears behind, barking—

Chomps down on the Giant Catatron's back leg, pulling—

The giant cat, irritated, shakes its back leg—

Maze can see below her the stagnant pool of water that used to be the fountain.

Rowdy keeps yanking—

The Giant Catatron scrambles backward inside the building—

Dragging Maze with it—
It lets go of her to snap at Rowdy—
But Rowdy ducks away—
And Maze tumbles to the floor. "Rowdy!"
The dog jumps into her arms—
Maze twists, leaps out the window—
Maze and Rowdy plummet—
The Giant Catatron explodes—
The tenth floor goes up in a burst of roaring flames and smoke.

While Maze and Rowdy splash down and down into the dark, oily water…

—

Across the wall in Maze's neighborhood, crowds gathered around the video screens jump back as the screens sputter and go blank. They look around in wonder and fear.

The little girl Maze helped earlier emerges from the alley carrying the box of food, leash dangling from her wrist. She giggles and lobs a soup can at a video screen. The screen cracks.

—

Later that morning, Jayks stands amid the smoking debris and wreckage of Nation Headquarters. Guards and cops sift through, looking for bodies. A shout, and two guards carry the body of Trilla from the rubble and lay her down on the concrete.

"Another casualty, sir. That's three."

Jayks surveys the bodies. "All right. We're not going to find much more. Time to file the paperwork on this one, gentlemen."

He gives Trilla's body a final sad look.

—

Rowdy curls on a rag rug gnawing a bone. Maze, arm in bandages, gently rocks Frankie as she watches TV. Murphy sits on the bed cleaning a laser pistol.

On the screen, Jayks, now sporting a full beard, looks relaxed and confident for reporters. The caption at the bottom of the screen reads 'Presidential Candidate Jayks.'

"...and the elections won't be delayed much longer."

"Captain Jayks, how do you think serving as president would compare to your work as a police officer?"

"Well, they're not much different," he says. "I'll still be here for the people. All the people."

Maze turns the sound down low. Cooing and murmuring, she settles Frankie into a makeshift crib. She turns to Murphy. "Will they still come after us?"

"You mean is it over? Want me to give you the odds?" Murphy goes to her. Shoulder to shoulder they watch Frankie sleep.

Rainy peeks in the doorway. "Hi. You doing okay?"

"Yes," Murphy says.

"Rainy? Will you...?" Maze pauses, hesitant.

"Yes?"

"Will you teach me how to grow things sometime? In

the garden?"

"I'd be happy to," Rainy replies.

Maze allows herself a hopeful smile and goes to the window to look out at the desert full of stars.

www.ingramcontent.com/pod-product-compliance
Lightning Source LLC
Chambersburg PA
CBHW072111181224
19229CB00004B/73